Cyprus Journey
Zeno's Rock-Ola Year

Paul Pavli

To my lovely friend Anna
Please enjoy
Paul x

ACKNOWLEDGEMENTS

Many friends have helped and encouraged me, you know who you are, but I started with Janni Howker and the excellent class she runs as "The Writer's Toolbox." Thanks to Ron Baker at "Spotlight" and editors and teachers Elizabeth Burns. Especial thanks to the determined help of Isobel Staniland. Finally thanks to my brother for support and patiently setting up, redrafting and resetting the many and various drafts.

BIOGRAPHY

I am a London born son of Cypriot immigrants now living in the North of England in the beautiful city of Lancaster. I am a qualified Psychotherapist and have written numerous articles for professional journals. Father to two children, hobbies include cooking mainly Cypriot classics, dancing Tango and hoping that this year will be the year when Tottenham Hotspur win. Something.

Webpage : paulpavli.co.uk

Email :paul_pavli@yahoo.co.uk

Edition 1 2017

CHAPTER ONE

I told Mum I couldn't do up the top button on the new blue trousers she bought me for the trip, made with slippery, "easy wash" material.

"Leave it, leave it undone, Zeno. And remember there are snakes, always make noise when you walk in the fields. Always. Don't forget eh? And hurry up, finish packing, the taxi will be here soon."

I knew about the snakes, Mum kept on about them, but a taxi? I'd never been in a taxi before. At least that will be something good. It didn't take me long to finish my packing. The canvas bag had a few of my less holey socks, two changes of underpants, my school shirt that was for best and another pair of trousers. Mum said that there would be plenty of boy's clothes that I could use when I got there, but Dad said they would need to be man sized. I was allowed two books only, so I took *"Billy Bunter goes to Brazil"* and my favourite *"Just William."*

Maria knocked on my door. I knew it must be her. A few weeks ago she said that we all had to respect her privacy now that she was seventeen. She got upset because men kept whistling at her in the street and calling after her that she looked like "Sophia Loren" but I couldn't see what they meant. She was just my sis. She had come home especially from Uncle's to say goodbye.

Maria helped me fold my grey trousers. Then she pushed something shiny into my hand.

"It's a long trip back to Cyprus what with the boats and trains. Get something with this, it's a two franc coin, a customer gave it to me. Use it when you get to France."

"It's got a hole in the middle of it sis. Will it be all right?"

"It's French Zeno. That's what they're like."

I asked her why Mum kept talking about snakes but Maria said not to worry everything will be fine. She helped carry my bag downstairs to the kitchen so I could finish breakfast. Dad had made some sesame toast with his special Greek honey that he kept hidden away. He said, "We should start like we are already in Cyprus."

Maria gave me a hug.

"Sorry Zeno. It was my fault that you are having to go."

"Never say that, Maria."

Mum came in from next door, her black dress crackling when she moved fast. She was still packing the suitcases with bottles of whisky and packets of tea. Presents for the relatives in Cyprus.

"We all thought it was a good idea for the business. Except your father. The only ideas he thinks are good are his own."

Dad heard her from the hall where he was trimming his moustache with his special moustache scissors.

He said, "Now look it's not my fault those boys came and anyway..."

Mum shouted back, "Anyway nothing. Look here is the taxi. Hurry up this is costing us money." Still chomping on his toast Dad picked up the two biggest cases and we went out by the side door.

The taxi driver sat in his seat smoking a pipe, his flat tweed hat low on his face. He spoke slowly to Dad, like English people did when they saw we were foreigners.

"Strap those on the outside. Understand?" It had rained overnight and there was a nice clean smell in the air, apart from the smell of the smoky engine. Dad opened the squeaky back door and got in after me. I gave Mum and Maria a final wave.

Inside the taxi a few chips had fallen out of some bunched up newspaper on the floor. As we drove off I started coughing as some of the diesel smell got inside the cab. It was like a really fat person must've sat on the seat because the dip was so deep, so I couldn't see out of the windows. It was difficult to hold on; the taxi driver drove so fast. He even went through a few red lights. We skidded round the corners, but there wasn't any traffic really so we got to King's Cross Station double quick.

Dad paid the fare. The driver asked, "What about the tip governor?" but Dad pretended not to understand.

I had to drag the cases, the hard plastic handle digging into my hand while my too tight trousers dug into my stomach. The station was full of steam from the trains but it wasn't difficult to find the right train in the huge station. You could see the bright clothes of the Cypriots and hear them shouting their hellos, "Gia sas" to each other.

A boy came up and punched me on the arm, his skinny legs poking through his brown shorts.

"Hey Zeno, you on this trip eh? I am Costas. Remember when my brother came round to see your sister? You are the boy that thinks he is English. I am with my cousins. It is good to go back to Cyprus eh?"

I rubbed my arm.

"I remember you, Arsenal scum and anyway I've never been to Cyprus and don't want to. Maria says it's too hot. And all you can smell is goat shit."

Costas started shadow boxing me, flicking at my face.

"You are ten years old and have never been to your own country? You will like it Zeno. We play on the beach and swim in the sea all day."

I aimed a kick at him.

"I hate the sea. I've paddled at Margate for about two seconds. It stunk. And it was freezing."

Dad pushed me onto the train. "Forget Margate. The beaches are beautiful in Cyprus, Zeno, and now we are free of English rule we can really enjoy them. Soon I will have all of you back home. Home in Cyprus."

I thought he was talking about all of us going for a holiday. But Dad had other plans.

CHAPTER TWO

Six months earlier me, Mum and Dad were sitting in the upstairs kitchen, trying to keep warm. Dad was making soupan for dinner.

"Boil an old chicken my boy. They have lived their life and have the flavour. Now break the eggs, make sure you don't get any of the shell into the mixture. Your mother will be like the cat that drinks sour milk if you give her soupan with shells in it." Dad cut the lemons. "Now come and squeeze the lemons. You like doing that eh?"

I went and got the glass lemon squeezer from the cupboard. It was a job I hated. The juice always found any cuts on my fingers and made them sting. But it kept Dad happy. And that might mean a few bob in pocket money.

Mum turned the pages of the big green book that had all the money from the Café written down. She rubbed her feet. She suffered with her feet.

"Manoli, we have to do something, we only made twenty-five pounds, nine shillings and sixpence last week. You are not interested in the business. Only you are in the kitchen cooking, cooking, always cooking, food they don't want."

Maria came in after watching the end of 'Juke Box Jury.' That's when she had her good idea.

"Mum's right, Dad. You cook all that Greek

stuff and all they want is egg and chips or sausage and chips or just chips. Anyway I know what would bring people in. A jukebox. The café down the road has one and they are packed all the time."

Dad scratched his bald head, never a good sign.

"Music? You want to play music? I am a cook. The English should come to eat my food, Cypriot food, the best."

"Dad, listen for once. Last week a man came into my Salon. He was from the jukebox company. He said it was cheap to rent. Maybe if you had one, young people would come into your café instead of all the usual old codgers."

"Look, if they want to listen to music let them put the radio on." He banged the metal spoon on the table. "And always I tell you Maria mou. Don't speak English upstairs. Greek here. English downstairs."

"Getting a jukebox? Daddy-oh. Cool." Pedri had come into the kitchen bouncing on his toes, like in '77 Sunset Strip'. Pedri liked Kookie and pretended he was just like him, always combing his bouncy hair. I wanted to be Effraim Zimbalist Jr. But what kind of name is that?

"A jukebox would help me with my band practice."

"You need to practise too," I said it double quick and then dived behind Maria. Even though he was a year older than Maria he never slapped me when she was around.

Mum slammed the book shut.

"If it helps with Pedriti's music that will

make us rich one day then we must get one. Maria, don't listen to your father. Get this man to come here. But do not be alone with him eh?"

There's no arguing with Mum when she makes up her mind, but Dinos was worried when he heard about it the next day. I told him about it when he was helping me with my homework. He said it was his job as my older brother to get me through the exam.

"What is this 11 plus anyway Den?"

Dinos took off his new 'Michael Caine' glasses that he now wore all the time.

"Next year you need to pass it, Zeno, to go to the best school, not the crapheap I went to."

"It's all so boring, Den. I know the Catholics followed the Pope, who was bad because he wanted to invade England, and that Protestants followed God, but I thought it was the same God as Catholics; or was it a different one? And how did the King of Spain fit in with all this? I knew he wasn't the Pope and the Pope wasn't a King. Sod it. What about this jukebox idea anyway?"

"Don't try and change the subject, Zen. All I know is that I want to be there when the jukebox man comes. I'm not getting stuffed for no jukebox like I got talked into getting the television from Radio Rentals. Just because I am twenty-one. Dad hadn't wanted that either so it was muggins here that had to pay every week. Never again."

"Dad doesn't want it. He said he wants everybody to come and eat his food not listen to music."

"He wants everybody to eat moussaka and kleftico not egg and chips which is what they want. His food is not making us any money even though it's good. Now no more messing. Let's get this homework done."

CHAPTER THREE

The day the jukebox man came I made sure I was downstairs in the café. I was trying to see if I could get to the till to see if I could lift a few bob, but Mum was on the prowl. Maria swished through the bead curtain that separated the kitchen from the café, wearing her new red dress, the one with a black belt tight round her waist. She went to wipe the steamy windows of the café and then we heard a van outside. Looking out I saw a Bedford van with a "Rock-Ola" sign bright on its side. Two men got out: one went to the back of the van to open the doors; the younger, who was squeezed into a bright blue suit, came in to the cafe. As he walked past I smelt a sharp, sweet smell.

As I sniffed Maria whispered, "Old Spice after shave." She called out to Dad, "The man from the jukebox company has come." Like she knew who he was already. Dad came out of the kitchen, wiping his hands on a clean white towel. Mum wanted him to use paper ones, they were cheaper and meant less washing up, but Dad said all proper cooks used real towels not bits of paper.

The young man walked up to Dad reading from a piece of paper. He went to shake Dad's hand. "Er Mr Anthony, I am Steven Wilson, from The ROCK-OLA Jukebox Company. Just call me

Steve."

Dad gripped Steve's hand. "And I am Antoniou not Anthony. You can call me Mr Antoniou. Please tell me what you have to tell me. I am busy."

"So Mr Antoniou this is the 1495 model. The best we've got, two-hundred selections, multiple play features and at low monthly cost too. Turnover will increase by fifty-percent with this model." The other man had wheeled the big machine through the café door and plugged it in.

"My friend, the fox can hear the rabbit when he is under his feet," Dad said. "I know what you are telling me. You say 'turnover'? But turnover of what? Cup of coffee here, ham sandwich there... If they come and listen to music they will not eat. It's nothing."

Everybody was looking at the jukebox, so I sneaked a Robertson's apple and blackberry fruit pie, my favourite from the counter. I would have to wait to bite into its crispy sweetness.

Mum and Dad were arguing, Maria was doing that tilting-head, stretching out thing that girls do, then Dad said he'd had enough. He didn't care. The women could get the jukebox. What difference would it make? Mum followed him into the kitchen to carry on the argument so Steve showed Maria how to choose a record, the arm swinging round to play with a hiss. Their heads touched; the blue of his suit and the red of Maria's dress bright as the lights of the jukebox. Maria found the square gold buttons hard to press, so he put his hand over hers to help her. They put on a song with that line, "Don't walk away, hey, OK."

Mum came back into the café still arguing with Dad.

"Cook your own onions with the fat from your stomach. Don't bother me with any onions anymore." Mum wasn't good at frying onions. You always knew it was Mum because she fried them too quickly and they had that sharp burnt smell. She saw Steve and Maria together.

"Why is this man still here? I told you not to be alone with him. Now send him away. You are like a dripping watermelon ripe for a man to bite into you. It's time to get you married to a nice Cypriot boy."

Steve didn't need to understand Greek. He saw the look on Mum's face and got out sharpish. He gave me a wink as he bustled out. I winked back. Mum followed him out so didn't hear Maria mumble, "A Cypriot boy? Over my dead body."

I didn't think a jukebox would help me at school. There was no point trying to pay off Keith 'The Beast' Williams with music. He wanted money. And he wanted it now.

CHAPTER FOUR

Next Monday morning, still cold, the frost making swirly patterns inside the roof window of my bedroom. I shared it with Pedri, but his bed was empty. He hadn't come home again. Often he stayed at his friend's house. He said he didn't want to share a room that stunk of my farts, but *he* could talk. He used to blow one out on purpose, at least mine came out by accident, well most of the time. What I smelt now was toast. That would be Dinos'. He liked toast and cheese in the mornings.

Maria was shouting up the stairs at me."Zeno, shift that body of yours or I'll come and shift it for you. Give Pedri a shove too, he's late." Maria had a way of twisting your ear to get you up so I pulled on my grey school trousers that were on the floor and my shirt, tie and jumper that I had kept under the blankets. I went downstairs; Dad's jacket was gone. Sometimes he went early to the market to get supplies; so no chance of finding some loose change in his pocket. It looked like the only money I would have to give 'The Beast' would be dinner money.

Maria and Dinos were talking quietly in the kitchen.

"Dinos, it would kill the old witch if Pedri got a flat."

I had heard Pedri talking about how he wanted to move out. Maybe I would get my own room now.

"What flat is Pedri getting, Maria?"

"For a big boy you move around quietly don't you? Anyway this is no business for a ten-year-old."

Maria was cutting up a grapefruit. She hadn't been bringing me any sweets or giving me some of her special end of week Mars Bars since she started this latest diet. It had to stop.

I picked up a slice of grapefruit.

"Sis, you are going to turn yellow if you eat any more of these."

"What's it to you, Mr. Well Dressed of 1963? What have you got on? Haven't you got another shirt? And what's that mark on your trousers?"

Dinos got up and grabbed his work bag. "Leave him alone, Sis, he's a boy, he'll only make a clean shirt dirty."

"My other shirts got too small. I can't wear them."

"You've got too fat you mean. I've got some old white shirts you can have." Dinos always had a clean shirt since he started this new job at the town hall. He sounded like he was in a good mood, so it might be worth trying to get some money out of him.

"Er Den, I need some money for a school trip to, er, a zoo. Could you give us it?"

Dinos took off his glasses to give them a polish with the little cloth he got from the glasses shop. Nobody was allowed to touch the cloth. Or his glasses.

"Money for sweets probably. Bring me the appropriate letter and I will consider it." Maria's breakfast was a brown cracker that had cottage cheese on it. Pedri had told me that cottage cheese looked like what was on his dick when he didn't wash it. I couldn't eat any after that.

"Don't come it, Zeno," she said. "You told me you were going to the zoo last week. And this fucking house is bad enough without paying to go and see animals."

"Oh yeah, that was last week. This week it's, er…"

"This week its nothing, which is what you're going to get. Now have some breakfast and not so much of your lip."

I liked cornflakes with cold milk. Maria had hot milk on hers, but when I had tried it, they went all soggy. I liked them crispy, with sugar on the top.

"Zeno, you keep telling me you hate being fat, and then you put all that sugar on. Too much sugar is no good for you."

I did try having cornflakes without sugar. They tasted like, well, nothing. Like no taste at all.

Dinos got up to go, gave my cheek a friendly slap and said "Cheery-bye," like someone in an old war film.

I really wanted some more cornflakes. Should I pour myself another bowl? Then it was too late. I didn't hear Mum come into the kitchen. She could also move quietly when she wanted to. It must be where I got it from.

She started tiding up the breakfast things. "Don't eat them all Zeno, they have to last all week. Save some for Pedri, you know how much he likes that kind. Maria, why haven't you got him up? It's your job to help me, I have to do everything in the house and even keep the business going that your stupid father is ruining."

Maria got blamed for things nearly as much as me. She said, "Pedri's not here. He hasn't come home."

I moved out of arms reach of Mum. Sometimes she had a very long arm.

"What? I know what's happening. Some English poudana is shaking her boula at him and he doesn't know any different."

I was happy that an English girl's 'boula' was to blame and not me. I'd seen my cousin Evagenlia's boula but couldn't see what the fuss was about.

"I will go to his butcher's shop and see him there. He needs his own room. Zeno can sleep downstairs. I have to stop the English girls getting my boy. One of them will get pregnant and come here saying it's him. He needs me now."

CHAPTER FIVE

If I walked to school maybe I could save the 6d it cost to get the bus. It was raining that cold slushy rain, I was a bit late so I went through Woodside gardens, but you could never be sure there wouldn't be any Somerset Road boys there. You were safe if the parkie was around, providing you didn't walk on the grass, play on the swings or use the water fountain, but as soon as you were outside the gate he didn't care if you were duffed up.

Then, onto the high road and past the red steps and white columns of *The Essoldo* cinema, Dinos said he'd seen *'The Day of the Triffids'* and would take me to see it too. That's if he could get away from his girlfriend Judith. She worked in the accounts department and Dinos said she was good with figures but Pedri said there was only one kind of figure he would be interested in.

The 243 bus was ahead, stuck in traffic. Maybe I should just get it. But sixpence would at least be something to give 'The Beast'. Then I heard a shout from across the road.

"Oi you, Woodside boy." Somerset Road boys. They started running across the road towards me. I didn't want to be cold, wet, and duffed up, which is what I would be if I let the Somerset Road boys get me. I jumped on the bus just as it started to move. There was no room downstairs; it was full of women and small kids.

"Upstairs only please," the conductor said. She looked nice and if I played it dumb maybe I could get away without paying. I hoped the cigarette smoke would not be too bad on the top deck. The conductor bounced up the stairs. Please make her start at the back. There were only two stops and I might make it to school before she came to me. But she started at the front.

"Any more fares please? Have the right change please; I'm not the bank of England. What's yours, sonny?"

"Sixpence return please," I said in my little boy voice so that she could see she was putting me in the shit. Not that she cared. I let the big boys off first in case they wanted some money from me and looking out to see if 'The Beast' was hanging around at the school gates. I scooped in just as the bell rang. Second floor back was our form room: Blue house, next to the Art room.

I went and sat with my mate Dave, 'Sick Note' to everybody because his asthma stopped him doing P.E. and his Mum always sent a note. I poked him in the ribs.

"What's up, Sick-Note? What's first?"

"Ok Bubble. It's English. Have you done the homework?"

"I didn't even know we had any. Shit, that means big trouble for me. You know what he said if I missed homework again."

Dave picked up my homework book.

"Yeah, no more stupid lines. Straight to The

General and his cane. You know they are all going mad about this 11 plus. I'm a thicko, I haven't got a chance to get into the top set, but you and Michael have. OK, you owe me one. Leave it to a son of a desert rat. I've done this before. Hand your book in with mine on top yeah. Then just slip it out when you put them on the pile. Do the homework at break and you can give it to him at dinner time. Throw him a line. You found it on the floor. Any old bollocks like that."

We went into the downstairs classroom, Zash, one of the new black girls that came last year was already there, her hair mad, collected in rows of beads with two points sticking up on the top. She was big, maybe even a bit fat, but you could see she didn't mind. When Old man Rogers called her coloured, she said that everybody was coloured just that she was black and he was white and some people were brown. She looked at me when she said that.

Rogers was taking us for English. He sighed as he scratched his pointy out ears.

"Today, ladies and gentleman and those who are unsure, we will be discussing one of England's most famous poets. Often this is a topic in the examinations next week. Who has heard of Rudyard Kipling?" He looked round the room, the wooden ruler he held ready to flick you if you got something wrong. Except for Seamus: Rogers never flicked him.

Pretty boy Harry put his hand up.

"Was he really hard then sir, like a gangster? 'Cos you said he was ruddy 'ard. Is that swearing?"

Rogers threw the chalk duster at Pretty Boy. He often held that in his other hand.

"Idiot! Now, can anybody tell the assembled group about his most famous poem?"

I knew it was 'IF'. I knew how it started. 'IF you can keep your head when all about you are losing theirs'. Rogers often came to me when he asked questions, but I couldn't look clever after Seamus had told me not to show him up. Rogers had once asked Seamus what 'elucidate' meant and he said he didn't know. Then Rogers asked me and I said it was when you explained things and made them understandable. Rogers said: "Well elucidated Mr Antioniou." But after class Seamus had showed me his fist and said never to do that in class again or I'll get some. Seamus said he knew fine well what elucidate meant, but he didn't want to give the bastards the pleasure, especially an old pouf like Rogers.

Rogers looked round the room. "Anybody?" The girl swots put their hands up. So did Zash. She was sitting near the front with Mena.

"So the usual suspects have the answer, but let's hear from one of our newer members of this happy breed. Your knowledge of English literature seems superior to the natives. A native that knows more than the natives. Ha! So?"

Zash stood up. She looked straight ahead and in a clear voice she started.

" 'IF you can keep your head when all about you
Are losing theirs and blaming it on you.
If you can trust yourself when all men doubt you,
But make allowance for their doubting too;
If you can wait and not be tired by waiting,

Or being lied about, don't em don't...' "

She paused. I couldn't help it.

"Don't deal in lies," I said.

Zash smiled at me and then carried on.

" 'Don't deal in lies,

Or being hated, don't give way to hating.' "

Rogers stepped in. "Well maybe we should stop it there."

Seamus opened his arms to Zash.

"Sure the black girl did great. It's a fine poem. 'If' you get my meaning."

At dinner time, I caught up with Zash. She smiled that wide sunny smile that lit up her face. I knew I wanted to say something to her, but couldn't think what it was. She got in first.

"Thank you for helping me. I knew that you read that poem. I've seen you with the book. Maybe we could do some studying together for the test next week? See you later alligator."

Something was happening to my throat, a tight dry feeling. She walked away with Mena, leaving behind this clean sweet smell. My knees joined with my head and throat to go all wobbly. Dave was saying something. I had to really think hard to remember how to listen.

Dave started poking me in the ribs. "Calling Zeno, calling Zeno anybody there. You've got it bad mate. A bit of the old tarbush eh? But we've got no time for all this lark. It's P fucking E."

"And I've not got my kit Dave."

"Can't help you mate. I've got a note from my Mum."

Laughing Dave went off to see Welsh Mr Davies while I went off to the corner of his office inside the changing rooms where he had a box in the corner full of left over stinking shorts and smelly shirts. His 'dressing up' box he called it.

Davies was shouting at us to get ready.

"Come on my boys, shake a leg and let's get out on to this pitch. If it was down to me we would all be playing a man's game, rugby, not kicking a round ball around like nancy boys."

We piled out onto the muddy pitch, I'd managed to find two plimmies but one was too big and the other too small so I knew I couldn't run. Davies left it to Steve 'Posh boy' Conner and William 'Peggers' Peggerton to choose the teams. Both top boys on account of Steve's Dad owning a garage that Davies took his old Ford Popular to get fixed and Peggers because his Dad was something big in the army.

Peggers started to do keepey uppeys with the leather ball. "Come on Stevo you pouf, get those white strides working that your nice Mummy has ironed, or does diddums need a new hanky wanky. I'm having first pick."

Stevo grabbed the ball. "Fuck right off soldier boy. You had first turn before, now it's me."

"You fuck off ponce. Let's toss a coin."

"You can toss yourself British bulldog, I always lose. Let's do pudding and beef."

"Bagsy I take first step then."

"You can fuck off sideways, you skinny shit bag."

"I'll arm wrestle you."

"Let's see you try."

Seamus needed to sort them out, he was

always first pick anyway. They took turns picking until there was only me and Arthur 'four eyes' Blanko, half blind even with his glasses.

Stevo looked at me. "Not that fat spazzer." Peggers said he would take me, he needed someone in goal and I would do. The fat boys always went in goal, except Fat Danny who bribed everybody with Blackjacks and Woodbines from his Dad's sweet shop.
Mr Davies always said to shoot really hard at the goalkeepers because that was the only way to make them run around like the rest.

I managed to get in the way of the ball a few times, Peggers saying well done to me as our team won. At last it was over and we had to go for a shower. Davies said we all had to shower making sure we washed everywhere, especially our balls. "Look after your bits boys, they will soon be looking after you."

Break time, so I went to find Michael and Dave. I knew that it was also the day when 'The Beast' will come calling.

'The Beast' liked to be called 'Baz' for some reason. Nobody knew why and I wasn't about to ask him. We walked out to the playground past the swots who stayed in the corner where the staff room window looked out. You didn't want to be with them. In the other corner were the toilets where Baz and his gang would grab a smoke if nobody was looking. Baz always smoked his fag with the lit bit inside his fist. Like his Dad taught him from the Army he said. The middle of the playground were for the footie players.. The girls kept out of the way, in a corner by the staff playground.

Me, 'streak of piss' Michael, so called because well he was as skinny as a streak of piss and sicknote Dave found a corner to play our game of Jacks. Michael had got a new bouncy ball so he bet a penny chew that Dave would not beat him this time, like he normally did. That's if Dave's asthma wasn't too bad. Michael got first dibs because it was his ball. As we started our game the boys playing football beside us stopped to let someone walk past; someone that no one would risk hitting with their ball. I gave the heads up to the others. "Face up mates, we've got company."

"So what are you tossers up to?" Baz usually spoke in a quiet whispering way, so you often leaned forward to make sure you heard. That's when he could smack you one in your stomach. His puffy eyes didn't look at you. He often came close, holding you lightly by the wrist, but if you moved away he tightened his grip.

I was feeling brave so I spoke up first.

"We're doing fuck all Baz."

"So, Greebo, you fat foreign fuck. Speaking up for your poufy friends, the useless cunts. What have you got for me?" Baz came up close. He showed me his white knuckles, bruised by previous fights. They looked huge. I searched for some money, like I had some.

"Eh Baz, I've not got any. That is, it's gone." He looked at me, breathing hard. I could taste the early morning fag ash on his breath.

"Baz there must be a hole in my pocket, the money was here a bit ago." He was giving me his silent treatment. That was sometimes worse than him shouting. And then a swift, silent, sideways punch in the kidneys. That shut me up. I had to keep standing or Mr. Davies on duty might see that I was hurt and would want to know why. More trouble with Baz if that happened. Baz really liked to see people hurt. He liked to hear groaning. So I groaned.

"You'll have a hole up your backside where my boot has gone if you leave me high and dry again. Get me some money soon Greebo, or there's seconds. Capish?"

I was doubled up but managed to nod. The air got thicker somehow. Fear blotted out all sounds of football or banter.

"Here Baz, I've got two bob." Michael had panicked. He could have offered a shilling and then paid two bob. If you start high then Baz would only go higher. Even though Michael had paid up, Baz wasn't satisfied. He always kept you guessing. Baz put his heel at first lightly on Michael's foot and then pushed down harder and harder. He twisted his heel round a few times. I could see the tears beginning. I hoped Michael wouldn't cry. Baz liked to hear you groaning, but crying made him angry.

Then Dave stood straight and in a quiet 'he-knows-what's-going-to-happen-but-he's-going-to-say-it-anyway' voice said, "Well I've got no money for you. My Dad said I wasn't to be afraid of bullies." Baz's big head turned slowly around.

"So shit for brains, you think you have the balls to take me do you, you skinny cunt. Can you hear me? 'Ave you got balls or not?"

"I've got balls Baz." Dave stood there; just

stood. Baz put his face into Dave's and shouted:

"Well you won't have any when I've kicked the fuck out of you will ya? Not that you're using them for anything you pouf." A punch, straight and true got Dave right between his legs. Dave was standing with his back to Mr. Davies so the punch was hidden. Smart thinking by 'The Beast'.

"Get me some notes you spastic shitholes, as soon as. Or by fuck you'll be battered."

We limped into dinner. At least it was a good one. Steak and kidney pie with spotted dick for afters. Michael would give me his pie; he hated kidneys. That's if the pig-faced dinner lady didn't see him because she had her favourites and I wasn't one of them.

On the walk home I tried to think of a plan to get Baz some money. Even if I did manage to steal a few shillings, Pedri had a way of finding anything I saved. I tried to hide any money under loose floorboards, but it was like he knew all my hiding places. Maybe I should go the Dave way and get battered until Baz got fed up? When I turned the corner for home I saw the old Ford Thames van that Pedri's friend used to take Pedri's group to their shows. You couldn't miss it. The name of the band 'The Ghosts' was written in swirly white paint on the side of the black van.

I went into the side door and heard the sound of two boys laughing. One of them was Pedds. They were upstairs in our bedroom so I went to find them.

"You awright Pedds,?" I asked.

"Awright? Awright?" Pedri put his thumbs

under his arms and did a silly walk around the room, like a Pearly King. "You're a real cockney geezer aren't you, fat man. I'm not awright, I'm cool."

His friend Zack was with him. He was one of those skinny men that had a long throat that you could see going up and down when he spoke. He was dressed all in black like Mum. He joined in with the 'cockney' skit. "Oh mate, I'm up the bleeding apple and pears to use the dog and bone."

I ignored Zack and asked Pedri, "What you doing? Are you back home now?"

"No not back. I'm gone. I'm packing now." Mum had been out, I heard her slam the downstairs door. She must have seen the van parked outside. She shouted from the bottom of the stairs.

"Pedri, Pedri mou, is that you? Come and eat something and I will tell you how you are getting your own room. Zeno can sleep with your snoring father and me. He won't mind."

So that was her plan; like when I was a baby. Well Mum was going to get a big, big shock. I was so wound-up that I needed to wee, but I had to wait to see what Mum would do.

Mum bustled into our room.

"What are you all doing in here? Give Pedri some space. Look he is tired, he needs to rest. Who is this English boy dressed in black like he is going to a dead relatives baneririn? Why has he got a suitcase?"

I was still holding my wee, but I'd have to go soon.

Pedri didn't wait for Mum to finish. "Mother I have to tell you. I need to get out, I'm nearly 18, and I want to do my own thing."

"What thing is this thing? Here you have everything, food, washing; now you will have your own room. It is some English pudena? Are you in trouble? Who is this stupid boy, is he more important than your own mother?"

I couldn't keep it in any more. I better go to the toilet and anyway I needed to get out of Mum's way. She might find a way to make this my fault.

"How can you do this to me, your own mother that brought you into the world? No I won't let you."

"Yah, mother it's really what I have to do, please understand."

I was trying to wee on the side of the toilet so the splashing noises wouldn't be too loud. I tried practising, saying 'mother' instead of 'mouvver' and 'yah' instead of 'yeh'. It took a whole different set of muscles in your face.

When I went back into the bedroom, Mum was getting really crazy. "He's going, my baby, my best boy."

Dad had come upstairs now, as well.

"What are you leaving son? Well you know we all have to try and fly sometimes to see if we are an eagle or a chicken." Mum turned on Dad and said she was sick of his stupid sayings and if he was a real man he would stop his son leaving

"But oh no, all you can do is talk rubbish, as usual."

"It's one less mouth to feed. When I was his

age I already had a son."

Mum and Dad started slugging it out again, the usual insults. Mum was a hopeless wife, Dad was ruining the business, Mum should never had married him, Dad was tricked into marrying her.

"Well I'm going." Pedri took the chance to carry his stuff to Zack's van.

Mum changed her attack from Dad to Pedri. It was all out assault.

"You'll be sorry when you come crawling back to me. Only a mother really knows; only a mother can really look after you and when I am in my grave and you come to visit it will be you that's put me there."

Pedds waved her away.

"Let's go Zack; this is doing me 'ead in." He slammed the door on his way out. The house was quiet; apart from Mum's crying.

CHAPTER SIX

Dad said I had to help in the café because Mum kept going to bed after Pedds left.

"She'll get used to it," Dad said.

Business was getting better. The jukebox had started bringing people in, like the students from the local art college, who played Acker Bilk records. The juke box hadn't been much use for me. Mum said that she didn't want any of my noisy friends around, especially as they didn't spend any money. When Dave came all he wanted to do was keep playing Martha Reeves' "Heatwave." Tamla Motown was the best according to Dave.

Even I got sick of listening to it and Mum did too once she realised I knew how to play the records for nothing. 'Call Me Steve' had shown Maria the switch on the back of the machine that reset it and she had shown me.

Maria had taken some leaflets about the café round to the local bus depot so some of the black bus conductors started coming in to play 'Gossip Calypso'. Today four of them had come in, still in their uniforms. An older man, taller than the others with grey hair asked what the specials were.

"Is there anything with rice? It would be good to get some rice. In England it's always potatoes, fried potatoes, boiled potatoes, roasted potatoes, mashed potatoes; you can eat potatoes until you look like a potato."

Dinos took their orders. He was having to help more in the café, as well, though not for much longer. He'd said to Maria that it would be his turn to go next, and soon.

Dinos smiled at the grey-haired man.

"My Dad says the same thing. Well its kleftico or mousakka today sir. The kleftico comes with rice. Lamb cooked slowly with onions and carrots."

"Sounds good man and its good food your father cooks, but we like a little bit of spice in it to give it an extra kick. Would he be accepting for us putting a little bit of our favourite sauce on it?" He pulled out a small bottle of red sauce, but it didn't look like the gloopy tomato ketchup we served. "It's from home. We will add it afterwards. Please, we don't want to upset the chef."

The men all ordered the same: four portions of Kleftico. They went to sit down but there were only vacant seats by the window next to Mavis and Jessie, two of the regulars.

The tall man bowed towards the women.

"Excuse me ladies, is anybody sitting in these seats?"

Jessie put down her always lit ciggie.

"Looks empty to me. It's a free country, sit where you like."

"Would you mind if some tired working men rested their weary bones?"

Mavis looked up from her tea.

"You look like you have very nice bones and you can put them next to mine anytime dearie."

Jessie coughed on her ciggy as the men sat down. One of the other ones pulled out a flat metal cigarette holder and opened it to offer one of his ciggies to Jessie.

The grey haired one called me over.

"Excuse me young man, but are you Zeno? I am Zasherata's father. You have become friends I think."

Most grown-ups never looked at boys when they were talking to them. He did. It felt like you were special, not just a smelly kid.

Dinos came out of the kitchen and told the men: Dad didn't mind if they used their sauce. He cooked the food. They could put anything they liked on it. That was up to them.

From the window, I saw Maria walking down the street so I went out to meet her. I shouted hello, then I saw the Rock-Ola van drive past with 'Call Me Steve' driving. What was he doing here? She was finishing a packet of Maltesers, my favourites.

"How come that Steve is here sis?"

"What's it to you? Stop spying on me. Everybody spies on me. Don't you start."

"Keep your hair on Sis. I don't care. But hey, save us some chocs. You're always stealing mine, saying you're sick of all that cottage cheese stuff."

"Too late, you have to be quicker." She pulled them away. "Anyway, I'm doing you a favour; you shouldn't be having sweets. Keep your mouth shut and I might bring you some tomorrow."

As we walked into the café Dinos shouted:

"Hey, I need some help here. I'm doing all the work while you two stand around." He told me to get the coffees for the students. Dad had boiled some hot milk to make them frothy. He wouldn't buy a machine to do that. The coffee was poured into see-through glass cups that were bigger at the top and wobbled a bit so you had to be really careful carrying them. The students smoked stinking French cigarettes with a picture of a Camel on the front of the packet. I took each coffee separately so as not to spill it and then took them two rounds of toast with extra butter.

"Good work young man. Glad to see you pulling your weight." Old Bill was sat in his usual corner, by the radiator, his tweed cap on the table beside him. "Now, I did order a bacon sandwich with extra sauce a little while ago. Make sure you tell your father it's for me. He makes it just as I like it."

Dad was upset when I told him he'd forgotten Bill's order. Dad said he was a proper gentleman because of the old style suits Bill wore. Like the ones Dad made when he worked as a tailor. Dad had some bacon already cooked and made the sandwich straight away, with extra sauce. I took Bill his sandwich.

"That's very kind of you. Compliments to the chef, maker of the best bacon sandwich in London. Here's something for your trouble, I'm sure you'll be able to use it, if I know boys." He pulled out a sixpence, a whole sixpence: just for taking a bacon sandwich to someone. I could get used to this serving lark.

"Thanks very much old Bill, er, I mean Bill,

er, I mean sir."

"Just call me Bill. Nobody calls me anything else since I've retired from active service."

Dad shouted that two portions of sausage egg and chips needed serving. They were for Mavis and Jessie. I took one plate at a time. Dad said to hurry back so that the other plate didn't get cold.

"Thanks love," Jessie turned from chatting to the bus conductors. "Where's that handsome brother of yours? I haven't seen him for a while. Is he out playing his guitar, breaking some hearts?"

Mum had said not to say anything about Pedri leaving. She was sure he would be back soon. I wasn't sure what to say, but then Jessie looked away from me. Four boys had come in. They had greasy hair combed backwards with a funny bit at the front. Two wore pointy shoes. I couldn't see how anybody could walk in them. They looked a bit like the shoes clowns wore, not that I'd seen clowns, except on 'Saturday night at the London Palladium.'

You could tell the leader at the front thought he was the top man, even though he was shorter than the others. When he combed his hair, his leather jacket made a squeaking sound as he moved his arms. Dad had come through from the kitchen and was wiping his hands on a tea towel. He smiled at the boys.

"Well boys we haven't seen you before. Have you come to try some good Cypriot food?"

One of them, a bit pudgy, dressed in a normal check shirt, smirked.

"We're not boys, Greaseball. Anyway, we haven't come to eat any greasy foreign food. We just want to listen to the Jukebox. A ROCK-OLA, eh: they're the best."

Dad wasn't smiling anymore.

"This is not a dance hall, it is a restaurant, so please unless you are hungry go and listen to your music somewhere else."

A skinny one at the back, pushed in. He went to poke Dad with his finger, but was stopped by the leader, who turned to look at Dad.

"Of course, sir. Thank you, sir. We will have some tea and some of those excellent fruit pies, if you will be so kind."

The pudgy one stepped forward.

"C'mon lets have The King." He walked over to the juke-box giving the students a stare. As "Rock-o-hula" by Elvis Presley came on the leader picked up a sauce bottle and pretended to sing into it, doing that swinging hips thing that Pressley does. Dad was cleaning around where the cups were kept on the counter. The pudgy one smiled at me and shook his head at the boy doing the singing. The small skinny one shouted out to Dad.

"Hey, Greaseball what say you get some more Elvis eh?"

Dad banged a cup down on the counter.

"Right, do not insult me in my own business. I am not this Greaseball. Pay for what you had and go. I am going to switch the machine off. Zeno tell me what they have to pay."

I totted up that they'd had two teas at sixpence each and a fruit pie: strawberry, I never liked that flavour 'cos they had bits that got in your teeth. One and sixpence all told.

The leader got up.

"Well, as the tea was cold as a nun's arse and the fruit pie stale as one of my farts and as you are throwing us out, I don't think we should pay. Do you boys?"

Dad went and stood by the door.

"You do not go until you pay. You have eaten, now you must pay."

Maria came out of the kitchen, she must have heard Dad shouting. She said afterwards that maybe it would have been different if she had stayed inside the kitchen.

"Now, my Dad has asked you nicely to leave. We don't want no trouble. Come back another time."

The leader laughed.

"We don't make trouble. It does come and find us sometimes, eh boys? But hold up. What's your name darling?"

"It's none of your business what I'm called. So just pay and go."

"Suddenly, I'm in no rush to leave. Why don't you and me get to know each other a bit better. Let me introduce myself. My name is Robbie Dawkins. My friends call me Robber. I steal women's hearts you see. I like the look of your heart, both of them. C'mon just tell me your name and we will go."

Dad stepped in front of Maria. "Look pay and then go. Zeno, open the door to let the boys out."

I had to get out from behind the counter and walk past them to the door. I made sure to stand behind it so the door was between me and them when they walked out. For a minute they stood there, one of those long minutes. Then Robbie got some money out of his pocket and threw it on the table.

"Let's pay boys. But we will be back. Well, mysterious no-name girl, it was nice meeting you. You are tough. I like that. Let's meet again."

The skinny one started singing: "Don't know where, don't know when, eh Robber?"

Pudgy one said to c'mon now. The four tumbled out, Robbie smiling as he walked past me. He made sure to push into the door so it squished me into the wall.

Maria turned to Dad.

"We don't want them coming back any time soon."

Dad locked the door.

"They are banned. I will make sure they don't come back soon or ever."

CHAPTER SEVEN

"Maria, when are you going to be ready? They will soon be here." Mum heard about the Teddy boys, she said Maria was a danger to men and had to get married and soon. Mum had already invited some Cypriot men to come round on Sundays with their mothers. So far Maria had said no to the four that had already visited. Mum said soon they will not be giving Maria the choice. She had to decide.

Cousin Helen was round, singing. She was always singing. She said she wanted to be the Greek Helen Shapiro. We were in Maria's room, practising, with me doing the chorus. "Whoompa oh yeah, yeah."

Maria handed Helen another roller.

"What am I going to do Helle? I hate all this arranged marriage stuff, like we are still in some stupid village in stupid Cyprus. Always the Cyprus coffee cups, always the best plates with the picture of Cyprus on them, always the white bleedin' tablecloth that some cousin made for their wedding. Always wait to be offered the baklavas, never take one first."

"Tell them to shove it where the sun don't shine, darlin. I do. Why should you marry some dribbling Cypriot loukaniko? I don't mind a Cypriot boy, but he has to be nice. Now help me with this makeup. I want it black, Dusty Springfield style."

"But I'm fed up Helle. This place is a dump. Then I met that man."

"What man, Goru? Tell me more."

"He's gorgeous. He came in to the salon to meet his Mum. I got him to come round to the café. He sells jukeboxes. He smells so nice. And the way he held my hand when we choose the records. Why can't the Cypriot men be like him?

"You and your smells. So he pushed all your buttons eh?"

"I'm seventeen and I want to know, you know, what's it all about Alfie?" They started giggling, until they heard Mum again. She was hurrying up the stairs. Sometimes she could move really fast.

"Laughing always laughing, now for the last time hurry up. This one is a good one, why aren't you ready yet?"

Helen gave Mum one of her smiles. She said she could go a million miles with one of her smiles.

"So, Mrs Antoniou, who is it this time?"

Mum wasn't fooled though.

"Why you interested and what have you done to your eyes, they look like your husband has given you a good hiding, which if you ever get a husband you will probably deserve. Anyway since you are so interested he is called Vassos. His father is Dimitri, your third cousin on Auntie's side. They have three shops, one grocer's, one butcher's and one greengrocer's. So they have everything and no smelly fish and chips that you always complain about."

Maria pushed Helen out of the way.

"Well he will still stink. None of the horkades ever wash anyway."

"Well I don't want any of your tricks. Don't mess around again or there will be trouble Miss Perfect in Your Father's Eyes."

I'd had enough of this girl stuff. Time to watch some telly. The aerial was playing up again. Nothing I could do would stop the picture looking like it was snowing. Bonanza was on. Did they have cowboys in snowy countries?

I heard a car, so I looked out of the window to see if it was them. Hmm, a Humber Super Snipe, classy.

Mum heard it too and shouted to Dad to go and open the door. She went to check that everything in the front room was ready for the guests. She used the Cyprus coffee cups, small and delicate, the best plates with the picture of Cyprus on them, arranged on the white lace tablecloth that some cousin had made for Mum's wedding. The small forks that had red handles on them were polished for the baklavas that Mum sent out for, better than the ones Dad made she said, but I liked Dad's just as good. Mum made sickly melon gligisman, even too sweet for me.

I could hear them clattering up the stairs so I went to have a look. The mum looked hot in a giant fur coat that she was almost tripping over. The dad came next, holding an old style hat with one hand and pushing the woman with the other. Then came a pudgy young man squeezed into a blue suit like 'Call Me Steve', but this one looked one size too small. That must be Vassos. Then followed a boy about my age. That's when I met

Costas.

Vassos' mum gave her coat to Mum.

"My husband gave it to me, he gives me things all the time, I tell him stop, stop, Mana mou, you are spending too much money, I have everything and he says he will spend it all for me, just for me."

Mum scrunched the coat between her fingers.

"Some of these rabbit skins can look like real fur goumera mou and such good value down at the market where I have seen the Indian beggars sell them."

"Oh I don't know what happens at the market. Evangelina the dressmaker always does my clothes. Do you use her?"

Mum said she didn't have time to have a dressmaker as she had to work so hard.

"It must be nice to be someone with lots of time to waste."

Costas came over, punched me and told me he had three hairs on his balls and if you were fat like me, it took longer for that to happen.

"Which football team do you support, I'm Arsenal and you better not be Tottenham because they are all pushdees."

I told the gooner scum to fuck off.

I said "Don't give me all that Cypriot pushdee shit. You Cypriot boys just talk about pushdee and balls and girls boulas, nothing else."

"What else is there, English boy? Anyway, my cousin Nixca will let you feel her boula for a penny. I'm saving up to see what she would do for a shilling."

I told him Bonanza was on.

He thought Hoss was the best brother to have, not like his brothers who were skada on legs. I said I liked Hoss too; you could always rely on him. As we went into the back room to watch the telly I heard Maria coming down the stairs.

She was wearing one of her blue baggy work dresses, made with some kind of shiny material. There was a strong smell of really strong perfume, her turn to stink. Her lips were painted with red lipstick spread all over her face, like a clown. I looked at Costas. This we had to see. We followed her into the front room. The mother and son were sitting on the best sofa. Mum had bought it from a catalogue that allowed you to pay for it every week. Dad had said there was nothing wrong with the red plastic sofa that Uncle had given us, except it smelt like when you went to the dentist and looked like one of my nose bleeds. Dad and the other dad were standing. Dad had his special bottle of Raki in his hand and was just about to pour some into two glasses. It had to be special. That bottle normally only came out at Christmas or when Uncle came round.

Maria spoke in her best cockney accent, "Allo darlin, ows it hangin?" She went straight over to the baklavas, took three, without even asking and started to stuff them in her mouth. "Ooh pardin me eating these ere cakes, I like a good cake. I'll be fat as a pig soon, but then who cares if you are married you've got them for life then, haven't you?"

Vassos started laughing, a girly squeaky

noise. I looked over to Costas with a 'that's my sister' look and he gave me the thumbs up. Vassos' mother stopped in the middle of eating a baklava. There was no stopping the dad though. He swigged down his drink double quick.

Mum wasn't laughing. She came up to Maria and slapped her as hard as she did to me sometimes. Maria stopped, baklava still in her mouth.

The father was the first to speak. He poured himself another glass of Raki. "Ach daughters, I've got one myself. What can you do?

Vassos' mother grabbed his glass. "No more Stavros. We must go. They have let the old ways go. Anyway I thought this was a Greek restaurant, not how you say, an English greasy spoon. This is not what I want for my Vassos."

Vassos' dad said that he wanted to finish his raki before they went; it was good raki and an insult not to finish it.

Costas said to me that I had a great sister and I should come to his house so he could fight me properly.

Vassos' Mum was pushing him out of the door, when Vassos turned and shouted.

"Mum, please, stop. I know she is messing around. I would too if I was her. I don't want to do this rubbish being carted around and treated like some piece of meat we get at the butchers. It's good what she did, really good."

His mum took a step back.

"Vassos you mean you would rather have her than Katerina? Remember they said they would buy you a Mercedes. Any colour you want."

Vassos said he was sure; he didn't care about no Mercedes. But that it was not up to him. He wanted to let Maria say what she wanted.

Vassos' dad shook his head, took another drink of raki, finished the glass and looked over to where the mother had put the bottle beside her, well out of his reach.

We were all looking at Maria. She took her time and took a big breath.

"I want to say thank you Vassos. It's just that I feel like a piece of meat as well. I would like to get to know you as a friend but not as a husband."

Mum jumped up and said that she wasn't going to let any daughter of hers have friends that are men. They are only interested in one thing. Vassos' Mum said he wasn't like that, he was a good boy. This time Vassos let his Mum push him down the stairs. He waved at Maria who waved back.

Costas went to grab my balls and I gave him a final punch before they got into the big grey car and slowly drove off.

I went back inside expecting that everybody would be at each other. Mum kicked off first.

She said to Dad, "Well are you satisfied? I told you that you were spoiling her, letting her go to work by herself, meeting men, buying everything new when she will leave soon anyway. You have made her into an English girl, a queen. Now you will be laughed at wherever we go."

Dad took a breath to answer, but Maria got in first.

"It's not Dad's fault. I don't want to marry a

man I don't know. Someone that wants me to be a house woman, a yenega, just cooking, having children, pretending we are stuck in some stinking village drinking raki and playing that stupid tavlin board game. I want my own life. I want to choose my own husband."

CHAPTER EIGHT

"I'm forever blowing bubbles, pretty bubbles in the air, they fly so high, they reach the sky and like my dreams they fade and die." We hadn't seen the Teds since that first time a few weeks back. It was a quiet Saturday afternoon when we heard them drive up on their motorbikes. They parked up and bundled into the café, pushing their way past the students.

The one with the spotty face went over to the students, who were sat in the corner. "What are you looking at you poncey scum? Let's be having you. Go on clear out, this is our gaff. We don't want any Nancy boys listening to their shit records here. Scarper."

They all got up to go so I walked past the students' table to go and get Dad, but Spotty pushed me out the way. I stumbled and fell, crashing into one of the students. All four Teds laughed as the students hurried out.

Mum came over and picked me up. She shouted for Dad, he took his time but when he eventually came in I could see why he'd taken so long. He was carrying a big metal pipe, I recognised it because it was used to hold up a bit of the shed roof at the back.

He waved the pipe in front of Robbie. "No more now. I told you I don't want you here, you are to go all of you and you are to go now."

Robbie took a step back and then with a click, a shiny blade flicked out from his hand.

"See this old man. This is what talks now. You listen to me. We will go and be peaceable, but that will take work and work needs paying for capice?" He turned a chair and straddled it. "Now let's start with a little bit of something to wet our whistle. A crisp five-pound note would do very nicely." He motioned Spotty toward the till at the counter. Dad went at Spotty with the pipe, but as he did so, Robbie stuck out a foot and Dad went sprawling, banging his head on the edge of the counter.

Mum screamed and went to Dad on the floor. Robbie got up from the chair and went toward the till.

Mum stepped in his way.

"Now don't be stupid Mrs. Just give us the money and we'll go. Simple lines. We provide a service. You pay for it."

Mum wasn't going to move. She and Robbie stood looking at each other. Dad slowly got up and stood alongside Mum. Nobody was saying anything. In the silence, the side door opened. I knew it was Maria. She must've known something was wrong by how quiet it was.

"Hello? What's happening? What's going on here?" She came through the bead curtain and put her hand up to her mouth.

Robbie smiled.

"Our miss no name: very nice, very nice indeed. It's good to see you again. Do you know you might well have saved your family a few bob."

Maria looked over at me, then back to Robbie.

"What are you doing to my family? I'm going to call the police. Now."

Robbie nodded his head.

"Yes go and speak to my uncle Denis. He is the local bobby on the beat. He will sort you out. Why not come over here and let's get acquainted?"

Dad checked his head where it had hit the counter.

"Nobody touches my daughter, nobody. I will kill you first."

Robbie smiled.

"Big words Greebo. No more talking from us. This is the deal. Either you pay or we cause trouble. Take a few days to decide. Miss no name can help you as well. Let's see if she decides to be a bit friendly like. This time the boys were playing. Next time it's for real."

CHAPTER NINE

The next Sunday I heard the smooth sound of Uncle's Cresta, Dad had asked them round because of the trouble with the teddy boys. That meant barbecue time! We always had a barbecue with Uncle. They had parked by the time me and Dad got outside; Uncle puffed as he tried to pull a big machine out of the boot. He shouted to Dad.

"Come on Manolli, don't be a malaga. Help me with this; it's too big to get it out of the car by myself."

"How in the name of Maria the Blessed Virgin did you get this thing in?" Dad tugged at the machine, trying to manoeuvre it out of the boot.

"Be careful goumbare," Uncle shouted. "It's just come from the shop, straight from Germany where they know how to make things. None of this peasant barbecue shit, covered in blue paint."

They got me to pick up one end. Only when it was on its wheels on the pavement could we see it properly: a grey metal barbecue, full of levers and flaps, a lid at the top and a shelf that folded out on the side.

We tried to get it through the door. It just about fit, but wouldn't go underneath the roof where Dad had his barbecue.

"We must get it under cover, " Uncle said. "I

don't want it to get wet if it starts raining."

Dad stopped pulling.

"So it's going to be okay for us to get wet but not your new machine?"

"Look Goumbare, this has an electric motor that turns the meat just right, so all you have to do is sit, relax and drink some decent whisky. Not that you have offered me any."

"Goumbare you have to know how long to cook the meat for. A machine can't know." Dad tapped his nose. "Only this."

Dad went to the kitchen to prepare the meat while Uncle tried to light his barbecue, fanning it with an old tin tray. It was making loads of smoke, but not lighting properly. Uncle got some paraffin that Dad kept on the side and chucked it over the coals, making even more smoke.

Dad arrived with the meat, peppers and my favourite, mushrooms, which he cooked when the coals were hot: lots of lemon, salt and pepper. Yum! Uncle kept fanning at his barbecue.

"So goumbare what oil do you use on the lamb. I have my own from my farm in Cyprus."

"I know your olive trees; they were never any good. Now mine: that's what you call ellyes, best black olives with oil that makes your hair shine and your children strong."

"Ah goumbare, when are we going to see them again? What do you think about independence now?"

"Soon, I want to go. Soon goumbare, but how can I? I have two sons that are not interested and a daughter who listens to nobody but herself. Only Zeno is left."

Uncle looked over to me.

"Zeno what about going to Cyprus eh? What do you think?"

I said it would be OK, hoping for a sixpence from Uncle. They started talking about all that Cyprus shit: 'Do you remember the smell of the jasmine at night time' stuff. There would be nothing cooked for a bit so I went to see how the koftas were getting on.

Mum had her hands in a big bowl of mince meat that Dad had cut using the rusty mincing machine. She looked over to Auntie on the other side of the table.

"Lamb makes it too oily. I keep telling you it should be beef and pork that you use."

Auntie had bought her own meat.

"Beef has no taste gumera and anyway it was always lamb at home, why do you use beef now you are in England?" Auntie smiled at me, her bright green dress very different from Mum's all black. Auntie didn't believe in wearing black all the time. She said she wasn't ready to be an old woman yet. "Ah here is a boy that knows his koftas. You like the extra parsley I put in them don't you?"

I didn't want to go from kebab wars to kofte wars. Mum and Auntie fought about how much parsley to use, how much potato and if they should cook the onions before they put in the mixture or if they should leave them raw. Mum said cook them, Auntie said use them raw. They started to talk about the old days too, so Mum put on her Greek music. Mum had a stack of records that came from Cyprus and some new coloured ones from Greece, but she always put too many on The 'Parlephone' record player. The arm couldn't go high enough to play the records.

Still no sign of the koftas so I sneaked a fruit pie; cherry not my best but all I could get without anyone noticing. I went outside to eat the pie. Uncle hadn't locked the Vauxhall so I slid into its cosy red and white seats. When I was sitting in the car, I heard a sound that made me stop in the middle of a mouthful: motorbikes. The Teds were back, again

Robbie and the spotty one were on the first bike, Skinny One on the second and Pudgy One on the third. They parked up behind the Cresta so I ducked down to get out the way; putting my head right down on the other seat, squishing the pie as I bent double, the sticky red middle dripping onto the seat. They kicked the side of the car as they walked by, but didn't notice me inside.

Robbie banged on the door of the cafe.

"Open up, we can see you in there. We need a quiet word."

I peeked my head above the seat squidging more of the pie onto the car seat. I didn't notice that the pudgy one had turned round to look back at the motorbikes. He saw me, looked for a second and with his hand made a pushing down sign. I got the message and slunk back down inside the car. Then I heard Dad. This I had to see. He was standing in front of Robbie.

"You stinking shit faced diseased sons of pudannes. You think we are stupid to be pushed around? No more" He pushed Robbie in the chest.

Before Robbie could do anything Uncle came out followed by Dinos.

"I knew what to do with the fucking English in Cyprus and I know what to do now." Uncle had a big spanner in his hand and started waving it at Robbie. The women came out of the café as well, Mum holding a big metal spoon, Auntie a saucepan. Auntie pushed into the spotty one.

"Go back to your mothers and tell them what you do. They will beat you to make you a man."

The Teds backed off towards their bikes. Pudgy One said, "Okay, keep calm, let's leave it."

As they turned round, Robbie saw me in the car and spat at the window. They jumped onto their bikes. Robbie pulled up to the café door.

"You'll be sorry you foreign cunts, really sorry."

Once they'd gone I got out of the car, my trousers red with the cherry mixture. I went back into the restaurant. Dad was shouting, asking if anybody had seen me. Uncle was still waving the spanner around.

"They tried it with me, but I was a fighter in the army. The British taught me. Taught me good eh?"

I needed to wee bad and went to the upstairs toilet to get away from all the shouting. My hands were sticky from the pie. I washed them and looked out of the window by the side door. The Rock-ola van was parked outside. What was he doing here?

CHAPTER TEN

I woke up to the smell of smoke. Maybe Pedri was back, smoking a crafty fag with the window open. He did that sometimes. Then I remembered that he'd moved out. It couldn't be him. I started to cough. This was no ciggy smoke. This was something different, like that time me and Mum got caught outside when it was a foggy day. The fog filled you up all the way inside.

I tried to get out of bed, tried hard but couldn't move. My legs and arms felt heavy. They didn't really belong to me. There wasn't much I could do. I thought someone will come soon, but I just wanted to stay in bed and go back to sleep. Then I heard bells ringing and saw blue lights flashing into the bedroom.

"Come now, son quickly now." Dad had run into my room, telling me to get up. He struggled to half carry or rather half drag me out of the room. The smoke was thicker outside and Dad started to cough too. Why didn't he put the light on to see where he was going?

Loud footsteps came up the stairs.

"Evacuate this area immediately sir, we will deal with your son." I floated downstairs supported by two strong arms. We got outside; the fireman left me with Mum and Maria so I held Maria's hand. Dad gave me his herringbone coat that he used for best, but it was hot from the fire. Steam rose up from inside the café. One of the net curtains was still flapping in the front window, how did that not burn? Next to the window, written in white paint on the green tiles were four words. "Fuck off foreign scum."

Dad was shouting something, but my ears were getting blocked up with that swimming under water feeling. I felt my legs go wobbly, I tried to pull the coat up; it was dragging on the floor, the bottom getting wet with some of the dirty water from the hosepipes. I was still coughing.

One of the firemen told Dinos to put me inside the cab until the ambulance arrived. They opened the back door, I never knew that fire engines had back doors and I was pushed into the back seat. Everything was so clean and polished inside. Loads of coats, boots and helmets were hanging up with four huge axes clipped on the back wall. I suppose firemen need axes. Big brass letters said 'Dennis Merryweather' on the front by the huge steering well. I thought that was a funny name for a fire engine. No one would be Merry to see a fire engine would they? I thought what would rhyme with Merryweather? All I could think of was feather, but a feather wouldn't last very long in a fire.

Dinos got into the fire engine with me. I wanted to ask him what was happening, but I couldn't stop coughing. I could see an ambulance had arrived and had parked by the fire engine, its alarm still ringing. I noticed the bell was different and thought: maybe it was so that blind people could know what the different ringing sounds were.

The back door opened and a nurse smelling of strong soap asked me if I was alright and could I tell her my name. I tried to speak, but nothing came out, just a croaking noise. Then I started to cough again, really cough this time, one of those coughs that cut you in half.

Two of the nurses got me out, I heard one of them say, "He's a bit of a lump isn't he?" They were putting me into the ambulance. Mum and Maria had come over. Mum told Maria to go with me. Mum needed to stay because Dad was going crazy and might do something stupid. Maria was crying and saying it was all her fault, she shouldn't have got the jukebox in the first place then they wouldn't have come, but I couldn't understand why the jukebox would have started the fire. Maybe there was something wrong with it and that's why she had seen Steve in his van.

I must've been speaking to myself because Maria said, "Sure, sure, don't worry about anything, just calm down."

The nurse said she would give me something to help me relax. Maria was still crying.

"The bastards, they did it, I know it was them."

As I was drifting off a face floated into my mind, saying the same thing that was on the wall, "Why don't you fuck off home you foreign scum:" Robbie, the leader of the Teds.

I came around again to find a copy of the Dandy lying on the bed next to me. I didn't mind the Dandy, Desperate Dan eating cow pie, blah,

blah. I knew I wasn't in my bed at home. I couldn't move for a start because I was lying on my back so I was almost sleeping upright. Then there was the smell. Home always smelt of, well home, not this mix of wax and the disinfectant Dad used when he washed down the cafe kitchen floor before the health inspectors came. And then I got that I was in hospital.

"Hello can you hear me?" A nurse was hovering over me. "Do you understand?"

"Am I in hospital?"

"Oh so you do know English." She took hold of my wrist. "They said you were set upon because you're foreign, I know what that's like." She might've been West Indian, but I wasn't sure. She was a little on the plump side, but she was nice. She let go of my wrist. "Thought it was usually no Irish and no blacks, not so much brown people. Unless you are Indian of course, they don't like them either. Anyway you've woken up, you have been in a muddle haven't you, and no mistake, but we'll soon have you up and about."

"How long will I be here?"

She left without answering.

I was in a room with a few other children. The boy next to me had a mask on his face and a machine bubbling next to him. There was a skinny boy on the other side, reading a book. I turned to him.

"What's your book? Is it any good?" The boy turned his head so the sun caught his round glasses.

"It's called Scot of the Antarctic, about going

to the North pole."

For some reason Old Man Dean and his brain dead geography lessons came into my mind. Arc is north and ant is south. That's how you can remember. An ant is going south. So the Antarctic is the South Pole.

"Don't you mean he went to the South Pole? Arctic is the north, Antarctic the south."

He looked up from the book.

"You know you're right. I'm always getting them muddled. My Dad says I don't know my arse from my elbow sometimes, but my Mum calls him a coarse oaf. My name is Kevin. What's yours?"

I had to do the normal: 'I am Greek, but was born in England' routine when I told him my name.

"My Mum says there are too many foreigners in England, but I suppose you can't be a foreigner if you are born here. That makes you English doesn't it?"

I was too tired to tell him what my Dad would think if I said I was English.

"Kind of. Do you like adventure books? Have you read Treasure Island?"

"Yes. That's good, but it's made up. Scot of the arc or Antarctic really happened."

"It's hard to know sometimes isn't it? Like Moby Dick, how real was that?"

Kevin sat up in bed.

"Moby Dick is one of my best. I love Moby Dick. What are you in hospital for?"

I told him about the fire. He said he was asthmatic and often came to hospital. He hated PE at school, especially football. He was skinny so he was told to stay on the wing and just run around as much as he could, but he couldn't run around very much because he got out of puff.

"At least that's better than just standing in goal being target practice for a cannonball."

Kevin laughed. "What do you think, is it better to be fat than have asthma?"

I thought it better to be fat because you could always get thin and Kevin agreed. I told him about the Jukebox, he liked 'Locomotion' too, but his Mum said he shouldn't listen to black people, they were a bad influence. He couldn't understand why.

"Dinner time. Sit yourselves up children." A clattering and banging told us that dinner was ready but the stale hot smell made me feel sick so I said no to it even though it was shepherd's pie and normally I loved that at school. Kevin didn't want any either, but the nurse said that he had to eat because otherwise his Mum would lead her a merry dance and she didn't want any of her old nonsense to be bothering her; she had enough to do.

I heard Dad outside asking if he could see me. The nice nurse said that it wasn't visiting time but to come in for a few minutes. He smiled as he came in.

"How are you, Zeno? They say you will be here for maybe just one more night. That's good you stay here until we clean the house. The smell is too bad."

"Is Maria coming?"

"She is Zeno mou. She is here but one of the doctors wanted to talk to her so she is just downstairs. I know she is your favourite. She has been more than a mother to you than your mother I know. Now try some of these koftes. They were in the fridge so they didn't get ruined in the fire. If you were a bit older I would have bought you a nice bottle of wine, but here is some Coca-Cola to have with it."

I drunk its fizzy sweetness and straightaway I felt better.

"This is like medicine Dad. Can I have some koftes now? This is my friend Kevin. Maybe he would like some koftes too." Before Kevin could say anything his Mum and Dad came into the room. The Mum was round, dressed in pink and smelt of the stuff you put on babies, talcum powder. The Dad was skinny like Kevin and wearing a tweed jacket that looked two sizes too big for him. His Mum looked over to us eating the koftas. She made that sniffing noise that people make and called a nurse over and said loudly that the smell from the food of "those people" was upsetting their Kevin.

Dad clicked his tongue and looked up at the ceiling and then looked at me. I knew what he meant. The bloody English again. The nurse made Dad put the food away, no food was allowed from the outside, only food cooked on the premises. Dad said he had to go anyway, he would find where Maria was and why she was taking so long.

When they came back, Dad was shaking his head.

"Maria you know you must not speak to other men, English men, until you are engaged."

"Dad I'm not in prison. I haven't done

anything wrong. I was just talking to a doctor. He said he really liked going to the pictures and had I seen the James Bond film and did I want to go with him to see it? He was nice." She smiled at me "Hello Zeno love. How are you?" She couldn't give me a hug because she was at the other side of the bed so she just squeezed my hand.

Dad said he had to go, there was cleaning that needed doing after the fire. "And we have to think strongly about what we do now. Maybe like the Red Mullet when the food goes bad in one place we have to swim to a different ocean."

Maria went round the bed tucking me in even more. Kevin's dad gave her a smile and said nice weather for it, but he got poked in the ribs from Kevin's mum. She called him a stupid oaf, me and Kevin looked at each other and Kevin started laughing. He got into trouble then because his mum asked what he was laughing at? She said that his dad's loutish behaviour was no laughing matter.

Maria handed me some books.

"I went to the Library to get books that you like. Just William isn't it?"

I was really happy to get some books, even though I had read them all at least once.

"What's happening about the café, sis?"

"It's not too bad. The police aren't bothered though they say it was probably just a cigarette left burning. I know it was those Teds, but they're all in it together. I'm at aunties; Dinos said he was going to stay with his friends. He said he's not coming back."

"Sis, if you go then it's only me. What do I do,

sis? I don't want you to go." I was proper crying by now. I could see Kevin looking over to me, but then Maria gave me a hug, one of her best snuggly ones. She was crying too.

"Zeno there are going to be changes, big changes. I can't go on like this. But I will look after you, really I will."

CHAPTER ELEVEN

Dinos came to pick me up from the hospital. We took the 243 bus, but I told him I didn't want to go upstairs where it was smoky so we had to sit downstairs with all the old women and mums and babies. We got to the café to see that someone had tried to clean the white paint off the tiles. The front door was boarded up with planks of wood so we went in through the side door.

I said, "I don't want to come here Dino. I don't like it. Can I stay with you?"

"Zeno, you'll be all right here. It's not for long. I'll be back in the café soon."

We could hear Dad upstairs singing along to his scratchy Cypriot records. We went into the front room, the music too loud to talk over. Dinos went to turn it down.

"What are you happy about Dad? The business has burnt down, you've lost your money and you are singing?"

"Ah my sons." I could smell he'd been drinking raki again. "My sons, the Police said the Insurance will pay and maybe we can be free of this business, a new start. Maybe those bastards have helped us to get back to Cyprus."

"Well good luck with that then Dad. I'm off now. I'll leave you to it. Here's Zeno back from hospital maybe he could do with a bit of soupan."

I didn't want Dinos to go. Dad was in a funny mood and I wasn't sure where Mum was.

"Dad, where is everybody going to sleep? Where's Mum? When is she coming back?"

"We only need a small space Zeno. Pedri has moved anyway. Dinos will stay with his friends and Maria is with your uncle until we have space. I have cleaned your bedroom. Your stupid mother still thinks Pedri is going to come back so there are two beds in there. Anyway it will not be for a long time that we will be here. I have plans. Cyprus is free now. We have independence. We have our country back."

Dad had always gone on about independence. I'd asked Dinos about it. He said it was political shit, but not to worry, we are in England so it didn't affect us. I went up the stairs. I was tired. I sat down on the bed, even climbing up the stairs made me feel a bit puffy. It was nice and soft so it must be Pedri's bed. Before I knew it I was sleeping, I didn't hear Mum come in, but I heard Dad's voice, they were arguing in the hallway.

"Cyprus is free now. We have our country back. We should go back and see how it is now."

"You want me to go and sit with all the stupid women in the village peeling goutcha while you sit on your fat backsides with all the old men in the kafenion? You're crazy. I'm not going back to that life. No more for me. Anyway we have to organise Maria, she must get engaged."

"I will take her and the boy."

"You cannot take her by yourself. You will be

getting drunk with your stupid friends and leave her by herself. I would have to go and I've told you I'm not going back. She can stay. She will come back in a few weeks once we have cleared a little room. We can start the business again maybe even better. Turn it into a chip shop like my brother always tells us to do. Maybe Pedri would come back and help then."

"Pedri, Pedri all we hear is how to get Pedri back. He's a grown man he has his own life now. They are lost to us. So is Dinos. It is only Maria and the boy that we can save now"

"Well while you are dreaming of Cyprus we need to get some money. Why don't you go to Stomei and see if he can give you any tailoring work. We have to have some money from somewhere."

"Stomei is like the snake that starts slowly and quietly wraps himself around you and then he starts squeezing and squeezing until he squeezed every drop from you."

"Well there is nothing else. We need to have some money and that is the only way. Go and see him tomorrow."

"We have a little saved. If none of you want to go back then I will go just with Zeno. Me and the boy. Together."

CHAPTER TWELVE

"Hiya Mrs McShane." I was still off school after getting out of Hospital, so I'd gone round to Dave's and his Mum's warm kitchen with its smell of toast, old dog and Dave's Dad's rolled up ciggies. Dave's Mum was buttering some bread to make cheese and Branston pickle sandwiches.

Dave's Dad was sitting in his usual place in the corner of the kitchen smoking one of his rollup ciggies.

"Sit yourself down boy. David, get your friend some tea and a sandwich. I can see he is a healthy eater. There's cheese or corned beef. That's nice with pickle too. Zippo is it? I am sorry to hear about your father's business."

Me and Dave stuffed some sarnies in our pockets and grabbed a football to practise goalie moves. Dave thought he could be a good penalty taker; he wanted to practise his idea of looking one way and kicking the ball the other.

I needed to be quick to get away from Dave's sister Norma. She was 10 and wanted to practise kissing with me so she could be good at it when she met someone nice. Kissing meant her bashing her teeth into mine, rubbing her slobber all over my face and shoving her tongue down my throat. Kissing was rubbish but sometimes it was worth it to get some of Dave's Mum's crispy on the outside and gooey on the inside bread pudding with cherries and raisins.

We had to go round the back of Dave's flat because there was a dog that followed us if we went round the front of his block: Block Two on the Herbert Morrison estate. Cut through the garages, avoiding the broken glass and through the gates into the Ashley Road Recreational Gardens. Baz said only poufs and old dears went there because the parkie was always around, but that suited us. We kept off the grass as the sign said, but there was a small patch by the road that we could play on. Luckily nobody else was around. We had the grass to ourselves.

Dave whistled when we heard the high rattle of a Vespa drive up in front of us. The cream and purple shone; the purple glinting in the sun as little metal sparkles in the paint caught the light. Two headlights were bolted on the chrome bars. 'Sportique' written with a squiggle under the q, picked out in chrome on the side. There were two people on the scooter. A tall boy dressed in a green parka and a purple crash helmet, the same colour as the bike and a girl on the back, Zash, also wearing a purple helmet. The tall boy unfolded himself off the scooter. They walked over to our corner of the ground, Zash smiling straight at me like I was the only person in the world. She was wearing loose green, yellow and red trousers and some odd-looking shoes. When she got a bit closer they turned out to be footie boots.

The tall boy came over and did that special black handshake that Zash had shown us: hands together, then put your whole arm up, then turn your hand sideways.

"How are you boys? I'm Louis. Zeno is it? And Dave. Zash tells me you are her brothers now, her rude boys. You look out for her. I appreciate that. You help my family and I will help yours: simple lines. Now listen up. My lovely sister was a top footballer back home. Here she can't play football, it's all girls play hockey, girls playing netball. Only boys play football. It's shit. Now children some of us have got grown-up boys and girls games to play, if you get my meaning. So are you in? Will you play football with her?"

It wasn't so much asking us as telling us. Dave was the first to say yeah sure. I was still looking at the scooter.

"You like what you're seeing brown man?"

"Er yeh. It's nice. Is it the Sportique?"

"That's what you're reading on the side. You can read can't you?"

Zash shouted at Louis.

"Don't be stupid youth. He's one of the best readers at school aren't you Zeno? And he likes poetry, like I do."

Louis turned and looked at me, a steady long look.

"Poetry eh? Let's see if Shakespeare has got some competition. So brown man, what about writing me a poem? Say, about this thing here that you like. Let's see what you can do?"

When other boys challenge you it was usually about fighting or football. I'd never been asked to write a poem. I knew that I couldn't win on fighting, and definitely not on football but a poetry competition. I looked at the bike with Vespa written on the side. Something clicked.

"The Vespa
Is the Bester
Of scooters.
So you oughta.
Get one.
If you can."

Louis laughed. "So that's your poetry? Are you the whining schoolboy, creeping like a snail, unwillingly to school? Or maybe the lover: sighing like a furnace?"

"I know that. We did Shakespeare; that's what it is."

"Good work brown boy. Maybe you are worthy of my lovely sister's attention." He got hold of my hand.

"Now play well, we are all going back to Jamaica soon, when school finishes. Zash said she wanted to see you boys before she went. Now look after her eh?"

Zash picked up the ball.

"So are we doing three and in?"

Dave said we were practising penalties. Zash said she wanted to go in goal. I let Dave take the first three. He took it easy for the first one, but Zash saved it, no problem.

"Come on Dave, I know you're skinny like an alley cat, but put a bit more life into it."

Next one he did properly. She saved again. She gave Dave one of her wide smiles.

"It's no sweat man. You've got to play around in penalties. Do that little bit mental thing. That's the fun of it."

Dave had a new system. He put the ball down, walked twelve paces, looked at the ball, looked at Zash, looked in the bottom left-hand corner, took a run up to the ball and kicked it into the bottom right-hand corner.

Zash saved it, saved it easily.

"You have to do better than that my man. It's not where you look with your eyes that's important; it's what you do with your body that shows you which way you're going to kick."

It turned out that her dad was a big football coach back home. He used to play for proper teams and even played for the national side as a goalkeeper. When it was my turn to go in goal she gave me some advice.

"Anticipate, anticipate that's what my dad told me. Sometimes you might get it wrong, but even if they still score it looks like you're trying."

I tried to save the goals, but Zash was good, really good. Often we bumped into each other, falling over to land in a heap on the ground. Her skin felt so soft and smelt like clean washing.

Dave was coughing a bit.

"Boys and girls I'm getting pooped. The old asthma. Think I better get home. I'll leave you two to get acquainted."

It was dinner time anyway and starting to rain, so we walked to the corner of the rec towards some big concrete tubes, leftover from some building work, slightly damp and smelling of stale cigarettes. We snuggled into the pipes. Zash had brought a basket with food in it and I had the corned beef sarnies. She took out a bottle filled with white drink and some things that look like Cornish pasties. She told me to try it and smiled when I made a face because they were filled with a spicy meaty filling. It was good though. The pastry was very thin and had a sweet taste to it. Zash said her mum always put some pumpkin in with the pastry to give it sweetness. The white drink was sweet coconut milk, delicious. I told her how to make koftas. She said her Dad thought my Dad's food was the best this side of Kingstown. She turned to me and gave me a smile that made my tummy flip.

I said. "What's Jamaica like?"

"I love going back, I can see my Grandmother and all my relatives and swim in the sea and eat fresh fish. Do you go to Cyprus lots?"

"I've never been. Dad goes on about it all the time. Like it's heaven. The air is better. The food better; and don't get him going on the weather. He says maybe we will go this year."

"It will do you good to see where you come from Zeno. I always love coming back though."

We stopped talking.

We didn't look at each other for ages. Then she said,

"So Zeno what do you think of me?" She did that twisting of her body that pushed it up and kind of lifted her head thing, like Maria had done with 'Call Me Steve.' She looked straight into my eyes. My throat became tight.

"Eh? Yep, I think you're sound as a pound."

Time slowed down. The shouts of the small kids on the swings, scaring the ducks in the duck pond, all disappeared. The grass smelt grassier. The pipes smelt damper. I felt the heat from her body. She asked me if I had ever kissed a girl. I couldn't speak, just nodded. It's true I had kissed a girl, Norma.

"What was it like?"

I said it wasn't as nice as Norma's Mum's bread pudding.

Zash laughed, a tip your head back, close your eyes laugh. Then she showed me something different, as different as could be for the same thing. First there were the eyes. She really looked at you, a warm, crinkly look. She came close. I could hear her heart, or was that mine? The difference between us had gone and I wasn't sure where she finished and I began. Our noses bumped together. We laughed. With a sigh she found exactly the right place to put our two lips together, dry, light and electric. Our lips parted. Everything stopped. Just this was happening in the whole world. I discovered a new noise, a mix between an ooh and an ah.

Everything on my body stood up straight. I knew what 'doing sex' was. I'd seen the drawings on the boy's toilets. Now I understood what went where. I opened my eyes.

She said. "Your first proper time, right?"

I laughed because, well I was happy. Zash turned her head. "Shit." Had I done something wrong? Then I heard it too, the unmistakable sound of a popping engine, Louis's Vespa. As he turned the engine off, she took hold of my hand.

"He will kill me if he caught us."

"Zash, Zash girl, where are you? Come here now" The deep voice of Louis, close by. She changed from a goddess to a muddy-kneed kid in a second.

"I better go," she said.

I croaked. "OK." Why was my throat so dry?

"Look we are going back to Jamaica soon; so see you after the summer. Take care." She waited for Louis to look away then scrambled out of the pipe. I could hear them arguing as they walked off.

I sat still, very still. The taste of her lips and the heat of her body stayed with me. Boys talked about doing stuff to girls all the time, but nobody said anything about this feeling. I walked slowly home. Seamus and his gang were playing in the car park so I snuck through a short cut that avoided them, taking me to the end of the road where the café was.

When I came through the alley I saw the van with ROCK-OLA Corporation sign on the side. I stepped back into the alley so nobody could see me. The car door opened. It was Maria. She got out of the van, stopped, bent back in and kissed the driver: 'Call Me Steve', the jukebox man. Two of us kissing on the same day, me a black girl, Maria an English boy. If Mum and Dad found out they'd go mad.

CHAPTER THIRTEEN

"It's time you knew about the real world son." Dad said to take the day off school and go with him, there was something important he had to do. I wanted to go to school, every day to see Zash, but I used to like going with Dad to his workshop, before we got the café. We would go to have a cheeseburger at the Wimpey bar that opened in the market. Maybe we would go there again?

We took the Piccadilly line to Leicester Square, Exit 4, then past the sweet smell of the Chinese Restaurants.

A turn down some dark back streets, another small road then a crumbling door at the workshop, Royalty Mansions. The doors were open.

"This stinks Dad."

"The English do their business here, like animals. And they call us dirty foreigners. Acch."

We climbed 3 flights of stairs that had no handrail and some of the steps missing. On each floor there were cards advertising 'Young model' and 'New Young Model.' Pedri said they were prozzies, they did sex for money. One time one of the woman had come out of the door and gave me a smile. It was a nice smile. She said to Dad, "Is he your son? They grow up fast don't they, thank Heaven."

Dad didn't answer her but he got me a banana milkshake that day. I knew not to say anything to Mum.

Nobody was around today as Dad opened a door into a big room to the hiss of a steam press and the smell of Turkish coffee. Stomei, he owned the workshop, was with a young man who was waving his hands around.

"You are only paying me 2 guineas a coat, for all that work. Go shit yourself." Stomei was dressed in his usual shiny waistcoat.

"Ah here's the Professor, he will tell you. This is Morti Professor. Straight from looking after the sheep and ready to become a big business man. Tell him. Regular work, 3 or 4 jackets a week. And there may be alteration work. This is a good offer"

Dad shook his head. "Good offer? Two guineas and alteration work? How can we spend our time with Hong Kong readymade suits? The real money is made by the shop owners speaking, speaking so sweetly, but really the work is done by the Cypriots and the Armenians, working for nothing."

"Ah we have missed you Professor and your communist ideas. Some of us must be humble and get the work we can."

The young man shook Dad's hand.

"You are right friend. Just buy a shop in the west end and have some signs saying 'Bespoke' on it. Then you'll make the money."

Dad picked up the jacket the young man was

working on.

"This material. Look at it. It is so bad, why not choose the 14 ounce worsted, not this cheap stuff. It will last one year no more."

Stomei slapped Dad on the back.

"Cost, cost and cost professor. You know it's all about cost. Everybody wants something from nothing. Always."

Stomei was smiling and shaking his head when he looked over to me.

. "And here is your youngest? He's getting so big. In all ways. Is he as clever as his father? Maybe he would like to try and see how my watch gets wound up. We will see how clever he is."

He walked over to take his watch out of his pocket, pushing his big belly into me. I remembered he had done the same thing when he came to our house.

"It's self winding. You showed me before."

Stomei laughed and said yes I must be as clever as his dad.

"So Professor? You want the child to start learning the trade. It's never too young. "

"No Goumbare, never tailoring for this son. First I need some work while the Café gets repaired. "

"Yes I heard about the Café. Bastard young men here in England are not beaten by their fathers enough. If we did anything we would hurt for a week eh? Professor you know I would like to help you with work but you can see how it is. Even if I had jackets for you they would pay so little for a skilled man like you, the cloth would be so bad and there would be alteration work. Eh, I would be killing you with this work. Maybe try the Armenian, he might have some customers who are the top people who will pay the money you want. I wouldn't want to embarrass you with the poor work that we have here."

Dad said that he had a few other contacts he would go to, I could see he was angry, his bald patch always got shiny when he got angry. As we went to walk out Stomei said something about how he heard the daughter's engagement had broken. What was the story? He had some sons, they were idiots but good boys.

"I heard you want to go back to Cyprus, Professor. I may have some tickets but you will have to go straight away. You know how hard it is to get them. Maybe we could do some business eh?"

"Thank you, goumbare. Yes let's speak maybe we can get the young people interested?"

Dad went off with Stomei to sort things out so Mehmet the man who used the big press in the corner smiled at me and pointed to a box by the washbasin. I knew Mehmet from before, he was Turkish and had something wrong with his tongue, Stomei said he liked to help people who have something wrong with them. Its cheap labour said Dad. I knew what was in the box. Girly magazines called Parade. Girls in their knickers. Sometimes they had no tops on at all. Dave said I had to sneak one to show him but I never got the chance.

Stomei and Dad finished talking but it didn't sound to me like Dad was in a good mood to take me to the Wimpey. On the way down the stairs I thought I would try.

"Er Dad so are we going to the Wimpey? You know for some dinner?"

"Wimpey? Yes, yes let us go there. One time more. Why not?"

We were on! We bought some mouldy looking apples at the market before we could finally sit down at the brightly lit yellow Wimpey. I loved its great big windows and proper menu, plastic covered that had pictures of the different food. Not like our dark smelly café. I didn't have to look. I knew what I wanted. A cheeseburger, French fries. And a banana milkshake.

"Ach look at these prices, 6d for an extra piece of cheese and 2s for milk with some sugar."

Dad had a coffee only, he said he can eat back at home. I finished quickly. Maybe he would get me chocolate ice cream for afters. With the sprinkle things on top. He was quiet, like he was sorting something. Then he turned towards me.

"My boy. I've got a big surprise for you. It's time you went to your homeland. It is too late for my other children. Let's get those tickets for you and me. Back to Cyprus. Don't let me down as well. I'm relying on you now."

CHAPTER FOURTEEN

As you walked into Michael's house you stepped on a long plastic sheet on the floor. Michael had said to come for afternoon tea because he wanted to know about kissing. I'd told him and Michael about Zash. Dave said he wasn't interested in no soppy girls. But Michael wanted to tell him all about it. I had forgotten about going to his with all the Cyprus stuff. Mum had been mad at Dad for spending the money on the tickets. Maria said she was happy not to be going. And I hadn't seen much of Zash. She was spending lots of time with Meena and her other friends. I hadn't been able to pick up money from the café either so Baz wasn't happy.

Michael's Mum walked in squeaking like the plastic floor sheet. She must have been as clean as her house. She said "Would your friend like to use the lavatory before we start eating?"

I wanted to say that I'd had a wee before and didn't want to go, but Michael pointed to his hands and I got that you need to wash your hands before you had anything to eat. I knew that really, but we didn't often bother at home. Dad always said a bit of dirt didn't do you any harm.

I didn't like wiping my hands on the spotless towels, so I rubbed them on my trousers. She asked Michael if Greek people drank tea. Michael nodded yes. Then she turned her big head to look at me over the top of her glasses.

"Michael informs me that you have had an unfortunate incident recently."

I explained about the fire, but I knew she wasn't listening. She was busy pouring out tea from a white teapot that had a fluffy hat thing on it. Every time she poured a cup of tea she put the hat thing back on, then took it off again to pour another cup. She passed me a cup and saucer and I thought this really is like going to the Queen's. We only had old cracked mugs leftover from the cafe at home.

She said, "Would you not be happier returning to your own country?"

I thought I am in my own country, but all I said was that I liked it here. She said something about the burdens of Empire, but she said it to herself really. I took a sandwich from a pile in front of me. They were cut up in small triangles and had their crusts cut off and something eggy inside with little bits of green in it.

"Perhaps your friend would like a sandwich from this side of the table as he has eaten them all from his side."

Why doesn't she speak straight to me instead of to Michael? I must have taken too many sandwiches. But how many should you take? Is four too many? Should I put some back now? Or is that an even worse thing to do? I sneaked another eggy sandwich. They were nice. The taste went up your nose somehow and gummed up your teeth. I could feel some of it stuck on my mouth and I wiped it with the back of my hand.

She sniffed. "Michael would your friend like to be shown where his napkin is?"

I knew where my napkin was. It was on my lap. So I remembered a time in 'I Love Lucy' when Lucy was showing someone how to eat properly. So I did the same and poked at my face with it. Then the egg was on my napkin. Did I put it back on my lap then?

There was some juicy looking fruitcake and I thought I would have to ask properly.

"Please can I have a slice of cake please?" I was never sure how many times you had to say please and thank you. There was some kind of law that other people knew about. But nobody told me.

She said I "may" have a slice in a really loud way, looking at me over her glasses. Must be something else I did wrong. She picked up her cup to go out of the room.

"Well we won't detain you any longer. Michael has mathematics homework ready for the examinations. It is important for his career to have good mathematical skills, if he is to follow his father into the banking profession. I will just clear these plates away and say goodbye as I am sure you will be gone before I return."

I got the message and scarpered double quick. I made up my mind. I hated how the English did all this manners stuff. Maybe Dad was right. That Cyprus was best. If Zash could do it so could I. Anyway we were going in a few days. I would soon find out.

CHAPTER FIFTEEN

When we got to France, I used Maria's two franc coin with a hole in it to buy a sweet orange drink called 'Orangina.' It was the only thing that helped my sicknesses. Every bit of the journey had made me feel sick, the first ferry to France, and then France itself where everybody smoked those strong cigarettes. There was another smell, like when the toilet got blocked up. The funny upturned cars that looked like snails were good though.

I was sick of Costas and his friends as well. Dad said when we leave England nobody would call me names anymore but instead of fatso and greebo they started called me "English." Like I was too Greek for the English but too English for the Cypriot boys.

The second boat was really big. 'The Athenian.'

Dad said, "This is a good ship son, they will look after us here. The food is very good"

My stomach churned at the thought of going on another boat but Dad was right about the food. In the morning there were eggs and bacon as well as fruit cheese and fresh bread, as much as you wanted. At night we all sat down on long tables, sometimes spaghetti or other times Greek food. There were white tablecloths, wine and waiter service. I was allowed to sit on the big table with the men and not on the table with the women and the small children.

Dad brought me a book on the second day.

"Zeno you have to learn Greek if you are to do well at school in Cyprus." I went to Costas and asked him if there was school in the summer and he said no so I couldn't understand what Dad was saying. I tried to read the book, the letters were different from English so it made no sense.

Sod it. I gave up. Dad had never got me any books ever so why give me this one that I couldn't read? I was mad, threw the book over the side of the boat, it floated for few seconds and then sunk.

Stomei, saw me from an upstairs deck.

He shouted, "Now young man that was a bad thing to do."

Puffing on his cigar, he told me that he did the trip regularly.

"I get a special deal on the price, it's who you know my boy in this world, don't forget that. Now why aren't you playing with the other boys, getting up to all kinds of things, when I was your age, oh the stories I could tell."

"I hate their stupid games, pushing all the time and watching girls wee. It's stupid."

"Ah I thought you were different from the other boys. Here let me show you this."

He took out a small box, opened it up to show white and black chess pieces, I knew it was chess, Dinos played , he said he would show me sometime. .

"This is a travelling chess set, made in Japan my boy. You watch these Japanese, they are very clever people. Can you play?"

"My brother said he would show me."

"Well let a master show you. I have tried with my boys when they were young, they are good boys but stupid like their mother, they can't learn. Come I have a nice little spot where we can be quiet."

We went to a corner of the boat by a short flight of stairs to an upper deck. I soon knew why. He could watch the women go up the stairs. His mole on the side of his face moved up and down as he kept nudging me. "What do you think of that one?"

He lit another cigar, big and juicy like me he said, poured himself a drink from a flask he kept inside his jacket and got some salami out from a bag. He showed me the set, his big fingers picking up the pieces from the top with care. I liked how the set fitted together, opening out with all the pieces inside, and each piece kept in place by a magnet.

"Now let's start with the small pieces, they are called the pawns, they do all the work, they are the ones that get taken first. Even if they manage to make it through to the end they get gobbled up to be turned into a Queen. You don't want to be one of the pawns in life my son."

I couldn't think of the pawns without thinking of prawns, so that made me feel seasick again.

"Now the King and the Queen are the most important pieces. The King can't do much and makes the Queen run around and do all the work. But she has to look after him, because if he goes, then the game is lost. Make your Queen work for you my boy and you will have a comfortable life. My wife might be stupid, but she is healthy and strong and works hard and she had a good dowry. You could do worse than to meet someone like her. Everybody wants to be the King or the Queen but you know that's where all the hard work comes from. Why not be one of the other important pieces. The knight has a great time hopping around. I like to do a bit of hopping myself but maybe you're too young to know what I mean." He squeezed my leg, his face scrunched up as he kept winking at me on his mole side, making it jump up and down.

He saw a young woman walking by and whistled at her. "Now that's a piece I would like to play with."

Leaning forward I could smell his salami and cigar stinking breath, he put his hand over mine.

"Now this is my favourite. The castle. It stays quietly in the corner but it's deadly. People forget it's there and suddenly "poof" it gets you. Sometimes the best thing is to be quiet and wait. When I bought my greengrocers I let the other "pushdee" run it until it was worthless. But I knew it was a good business, right on the high road. Then when he was bankrupt I made him an offer, peanuts, but he had to take it. Now someone goes to market for me in the morning, someone else puts everything on the shelves for me, someone else cleans the shop, all I do is stop the taxman taking all of the money and have lots of nice holidays. Even my stupid sons will be able to make a nice living out of that shop."

He was sitting really close to me, his knees pressing into mine. I liked chess. I didn't like Stomei. Especially when he sat this close. I moved away from him so he sat back on his chair.

"That's enough for today. You've got a good teacher my boy, your father is lucky to have me on his side with this new business. We will play again in the village. The master has a few tricks up his sleeve. Just wait and see."

CHAPTER SIXTEEN

When we got to the harbour I smelt smoke, like I was back in the cafe again, but this time it was smoke from the quayside souvlaki fires. It looked like people were eating souvlaki for breakfast. Maybe Cyprus wouldn't be so bad after all.

Everybody wanted to get off straight away, fighting with the women trying to sell you things, mainly cloth and coloured cushions. There were some juicy watermelons that I liked the look of, but Dad said not to buy from people selling at the harbour.

"Water melons have to be given clean water to grow properly. Be sure about where they were grown. It's the same with souvlaki. Only eat the meat from animals you know the name of. Here it's the only way."

An old dog barked at me. I never like dogs and they knew it. Dad laughed at me.

"They won't hurt you here Zeno mou. You are safe in Cyprus."

We bought some fresh bread, warm from the oven, before a huge man with one arm, pushed through the crowds.

"Goumbare, it is good to see you after so many years. There are many changes since you have been away. I got your letter and we will talk later. And this is your boy? Gia sou, here take my good hand. I am Sotos your second cousin. Come, I have parked the truck by the market."

He was wearing a kind of skirt and his face was covered with a huge moustache. Dad was proud of his moustache but it didn't match this man's. It was really like a handlebar on his face. I'd heard them being called that in an old style war film.

We pushed through the crowds until we found an old Austin of England truck.

Sotos shouted: "Jump in the back with Angelos. Be careful of the chickens."

A crate of live chickens, clucking and stinking, were in the corner of the open truck bed next to a boy older than me, dressed in ragged shorts, with a red hanky tied round his neck. I couldn't manage to climb up the side of the truck and needed Soto's help. He picked me up with his one arm and threw me in.

The boy had to shout at me over the noise of the traffic.

"Gia sou, Zeno. I am Angelos. My father says it is your first time in Cyprus eh? Zeno, I am a cousin. I will tell you everything. But you must tell me about England yes? Soon I will go. Soon. My Uncle in Manchester will take me. You know Manchester eh?"

I held on to side of the truck as we bumped along.

"I've never been to Manchester, I don't even know where it is."

Angelos stopped me.

"Please not in English. I cannot understand

English. You can give me lessons yes? Just Greek now. Speak Greek."

I couldn't say anything else with the roar of the tuck as we speeded up. Also it was hot, really hot. I had never felt this kind of heat before. Usually in England I liked going out in the sun, but all I wanted to do here was get away from it. Not possible in the back of a truck.

It was mad getting out of the town, like traffic spaghetti. There were no traffic lights. Cars, lorries and buses were all fighting for space. Sotos kept his hand on the loud horn and squeezed his way through, even though it didn't look like there was any space at all. Soon we were out in the countryside. The road ran by the coast with the sea on one side and rocky hills on the other. The coast wasn't straight and pebbly like I was used to when we went on trips to Margate and I couldn't look at the sand, it was so white. The sea was a bluey purple colour, again not like the grey water I was used to in England. Some fishermen had found a shady spot in a bay and were fixing their fishing nets. They waved at us as we passed by.

The road got slowly worse and bumpier until it didn't really seem to be a road at all. There were fields cut into the hills with little trees on them. I asked Angelos what the trees were.

"You are a real town boy. They are olive trees, stupid."

I could hear some bells clanging and there was a sharp smell in the air that turned my stomach and kind of got right inside you. In the hills I saw some goats being pushed along by a boy with a stick. So that's what goat shit smells like. Lots of little white houses, single storey and kind of flat on the top were tucked into a corner by the beach. They looked like nobody lived there. The windows were smashed and there was writing all over them. I couldn't read much Greek so I asked what it said. Angelos told me.

"Fuck off Turkish pigs."

Raggedy men were moving furniture from one of the houses and as we drove passed they ran towards us. They picked up stones from the side of the road. And threw them at us.

Angelos pushed my head to the floor of the truck.

"Turks! There are still some here. Keep down." Sotos revved the engine and we skidded down the hill away from the shouting men. The road became better as we pulled into a small village. We parked in a square with a few other cars, mainly old Morris Minors.

Angelos brushed the dust out of his hair.

"Those Turks will have to be found and sent away. But today is market day. That's why we brought the chickens. Let us get you something to make you welcome."

We got out of the truck, Angelos took me by the hand and we went to a stall selling fried batter things that were dipped in a syrup and then sugar. They were great.

"These will make you even fatter, but we will get you working in the fields and that will make you slim."

Sotos gave the chickens to another man with a huge moustache so we got back into the truck,

Sotos again lifting me with his one good arm. We drove up a hill and came to another couple of houses just by the edge of the village. It was shady and cool even under the boiling hot, very blue sky. The little house was set in the middle of trees that had lemons on them and I could see some with oranges too. Just by the side there was a field that was filled with tomato plants. Dad always grew them at home so I knew what they looked like. The short fat trees that I now knew were olive trees were up the hill on the side of the house. A donkey was pooing in front of us where he was tied up so I became expert in the smell of donkey shit as well as the goat shit earlier and the sharp chicken shit in the van. Dad said I would learn about new things when I got to Cyprus.

Now something else was happening, I was being dive bombed by blue buzzy midges. My skin started coming up in big red blotches. Angelos laughed at me.

"English, your skin is no good here. But soon you will get used to it."

A mad looking black chicken came straight at me. Being chased by a chicken was something new.

"Don't go near Old Slit Eye" Angelos said "Especially when he's making babies."

I went through the shiny black door of the old house into a cool kitchen, a metal stove on one side and a white sink in the corner. Sotos came in and asked how I liked his old house. He had built a new concrete one over in the new part of town.

"Here is where the old villagers stay, not so comfortable. Soon I hope we will have a new road through here and I can sell it for lots of this eh?" He rubbed his fingers and thumbs together. Well at least that meant the same in England.

CHAPTER SEVENTEEN

"So what garkolla do I sleep on?" I asked as Angelos bounced up the uneven spiral stairs to the upstairs room. A small window in the corner, one single bed, a cupboard and a fly buzzing around: that was it. A rug on the bare floor had the evil eye on it, like one Mum and Dad had in their bedroom at home. It was supposed to bring good luck. A ladder going up to a door in the ceiling took up the other side of the room.

"What is this garkolla English boy?" Angelos said. "You speak Greek like a Turk. It's a krevati here. Anyway you sleep here. I am just next door."

I was hot, itchy from the bites, still feeling sick and the watermelon we had when we first arrived was having an effect. And not in a good way.

I said, "I had to go," to Angelos and where was the toilet? He pointed out of the window.

"When you want to piss, go on the chicken manure. Boys' piss is good for the soil. You shit there." He pointed to a wooden shed, painted green, by the side of the chickens. "Just sing so people will know you're doing your business. And use plenty of ash."

I ran down the stairs, hoping I couldn't hear any singing. The green door creaked open; it was a surprise that the toilet smelt clean. I could see the smoky bucket of ash by the side of the toilet that was really a hole in the ground. The Izal toilet paper on a hook was a bit of home from home, except that I hated the slippery hardness of Izal. Mum used it in the café toilets, but she had a stash of soft toilet paper that she kept hidden under the sink for upstairs. We were meant to use the Izal, but sometimes I sneaked a piece of the good stuff.

I could hear Old Slit Eye pecking around outside so I thought I'd better start singing. All I could think of was 'God Save the Queen'. Not that I liked the Queen, but it did the trick. At least Slit Eye moved away. There was a bucket of water outside to wash your hands.

As I walked back to the house a tiny woman, her face collapsed around her mouth, stick thin and shorter than me grabbed me in a hug. "I am the grandmother. Welcome, welcome. Come eat, you look like you need lots of food." I hadn't seen a mum around. Angelos was setting up a table under some shade by the side of the house. It was covered with a plastic tablecloth with different coloured fruit on it that was just like the one Mum had at home.

The old woman was standing on a box stirring a big blue metal pot, again like the one Mum had at home. I could smell something fishy and another smell, like the plants outside. She pointed to plates and bread. I picked them up and went outside.

We ate the fish stew with potatoes, hunks of bread and fresh tomatoes that Angelos picked, right there, off the plants by the side of the house. It was hard work eating the stew. You had to be careful not to eat the needle like fish bones, break your teeth on the olive stones or eat some of the leaves and twigs that spiced up the sauce. It was too oily and fishy for me and I needed to go and sing in the toilet again very soon. Maybe I could remember the words to 'Locomotion' this time.

When I got back, I saw Dad and Sotos driving off in the truck.

"They are going to the Kafenio," Angelos said. "First we help wash up outside with a kettle of hot water. Like we are girls."

The grandmother gave Angelos a play slap, hardly reaching his head.

"When you earn some money for the family you can be a man, but until then, you wash up."

Angelos started clattering with the pans.

"C'mon Zeno, time to help now. I will take you to the village once we have finished. I know a short cut. You can learn how to climb and jump to get to places quickly."

After finishing off the plates, we set off, climbing over a fallen tree, jumping over a big hole and squeezing through some rocks. Angelos didn't look like he touched the ground as he walked, but I dragged half of the ground along with me.

The Kafenio was in the centre of the village, on the shady side of the market square. I was glad to see it because I needed the toilet again, fast. This time the toilet stunk and only had newspaper for toilet paper, but at least it had a chain to pull.

The men were drinking hot sweet coffee and Dad's special gobstopper smelling drink called raki. When Dad had some at home he started singing his old Cypriot songs. There was already a man in the corner singing in that shouting Greek way, so maybe Dad wouldn't start. The singer was on a little stage made of Coca-Cola boxes and was playing the round backed guitar that Dad wanted Pedri to play. "Over my dead body," Pedri had said. The walls were covered in pictures; Jimmy Greaves was there next to Archbishop Makarios. The biggest picture was a man with a big moustache in an Army uniform.

"Who's the army guy?" I asked Angelos.

He punched my arm.

"It's General Grevas. Don't they teach you anything in English schools? He got rid of the English. Along with my Dad."

"Your Dad fought the English?"

"Where do you think his arm went? Phiff, a bullet, he was put in prison and the doctor couldn't save it. That's why he can't go to England. They won't let him because of the prison record. Unless he goes as someone else but only having one arm makes that difficult."

The air was thick with cigarette smoke, so I couldn't be in there very long. Dad was playing tavlin with Sotos both of them sitting outside under a vine, like Dad had at home. Only ten times bigger. Dad had tried to teach me tavlin. It's called backgammon in English he said. I never got the hang of it.

I went over to Dad but he didn't see me. He and Sotos were talking.

"It is too high gumbare. We could never build a house there."

Sotos waved his good arm and said they could put a road at the bottom of the hill and build steps to a house.

"You will have a beautiful view and a fresh wind to keep the bastard mosquitoes from biting you." He squished one of the midges with a lightening flick of his good arm. Maybe having one arm made you able to use it really quickly?

Dad hadn't seen me so he was surprised when I said, "What new house?"

"It's not something to talk about now," Dad said. "Soon, soon you will know. Now have a Coca. But not with ice. It comes from bad water and will give you a bad stomach." I had that already so I didn't think ice would make any difference.

After I got the Coca Angelos came and found me. "Hey Zeno, here's Fanoula, she will tell you all that boys need to know." Angelos waved me over to a woman serving drinks, with a bright red headscarf on. The rest of her looked like she was all bosoms. "Fanoula here's a boy from England. Zeno Antionou. He doesn't know what women have got that men want."

Fanoula turned round, with her dark, almost black eyes. She looked straight at me, deep inside.

"Zeno? So you want me to tell him? Well let's see what I can tell him. About women? Let him go and watch his sister when she is taking a bath. Now go away I am busy with real men."

I was really tired by now so I couldn't talk about Zash. It was really loud and noisy in the Kafenio, I couldn't speak to Dad, then Sotos found me to say Yiannis, another cousin was driving back and could give me and Angelos a lift. I was so tired I almost fell asleep in the rattly truck as we bumped our way home. Tomorrow Angelos said I needed to get to know the other boys in the village. First I needed to sleep.

CHAPTER EIGHTEEN

I woke up hearing the chickens fussing and clucking outside. I really was in Cyprus. I wanted one of Dave's dad's crispy bacon sarnies, soaked in brown sauce, followed by a gooey Robertson's apple and blackcurrant pie. But there was no smell of cooking bacon.

Angelos shouted from downstairs.

"There are some old clothes of my cousin that should fit you. He was big. Try them." I saw a faded green shirt and some grey shorts on the bed. They fitted fine so I went downstairs and then outside to the table under the vine tree.

Angelos was laying out some bowls on the table.

"This morning you slept, but tomorrow you work with me. We have to get the eggs from the chickens without Slit Eye seeing us and collect the honey from the bees and also clean up the donkeys."

I needed to go to the green shed so I waved my arms and shouted poudana, malaga, pushdee at Slit Eye when he came towards me. They were all the Greek swear words I knew. Looked like he knew them too as he high stepped his way back to the hens. I remembered to go and wee in the compost heap and not the green shed.

There was food outside on the table, but it

looked suspiciously like the yoghurt Maria had when she was on a diet. The old lady offered me some.

I shook my head. "No thanks. I hate this stuff, it squeezes your mouth when you eat it."

Angelos put some on a plate.

"Try it Zeno. And remember only Greek now. The yoghurt is straight from the mountain sheep. Sweet it up with honey. I will show you where honey comes from. You can help me collect it." Another thing to learn. I didn't want to collect no honey. I'd been stung by bees a few times and I didn't fancy being stung again. There was watermelon and another purple fruit that I hadn't seen. Angelos saw me looking at them.

"They are figs Zeno. Try. Try everything."

I bit into the purple skin. Sweet, juicy and full of little seeds: delicious. And then there was a boiled egg. Boiled eggs are rubbish at home, a way of eating toast. This egg was different. It looked different. The yellow bit was really yellow. And it smelt of, well, egg. The white was so creamy and the yellow bounced with taste. I wanted another one.

Angelos said. "You can't expect the girls to lay more just for you. If they lay more you have more. If they lay none you have none. It's simple here." Dad had already gone off somewhere. Breakfast was over. Now what?

Angelos packed some bread, olives and tomatoes in a bag with a tin of something.

"Now come with me. Let's go and meet the boys."

We took another short cut, this time a simple

walk through some rocks. Then onto the widest,, sandiest beach and bluest sea I had ever seen. Five or six boys were kicking a ball around by the side of the sea. Costas was with them, arguing as usual.

"Why can't I be the first one? I'm the best; can't you see you malagas?"

"Boys, here's someone from England. He is Zeno Antionou. He is fat and English but a good boy. It is his first time in his home country. Let's show him what is it is like to be really Cypriot."

Costas came running up and this time I punched him first.

"That's good Zeno." Angelos laughed. "You are learning already. If someone looks like they will hit you, hit them first. That is the Cypriot way. But first you have to learn how to punch like a man, not a pushdee."

Angelos held my arm.

"First keep your thumb outside of your hand, keep the wrist straight and punch from your body not from the arm."

Everybody started practising so it ended up with a bundle. After we stopped a tall boy with the hairiest legs I had ever seen asked me in his bad English. "And you, Zeno, from England where they think they can play football. What team do you support? Tottingham is the team for us here. They have the best players." I told them it's called Tottenham, not Tottingham and maybe if they wanted me to learn Greek they should learn English as well.

The hairy boy told me he was called Vassos; maybe I could give him English lessons. I said

Angelos wants some too.

"Maybe I will set up a school?"

"Manchester are the best team." A fair haired small boy bounced a ball as best he could on a hard bit of the beach. "I will go there when I go to England. Now let's play. It is better to play football than talk about it. Where do you play Tottenham man? You cannot run so we must put you in goal. That's where all the fat boys play."

They were playing attack v defence, so they only needed one goalkeeper. This was my chance to show off everything Zash had shown me. I took my time organising the goal posts which were made up of old bits of stick and rocks from the beach. I made sure I could see where the penalty area was, just like Zash had shown me. And then I did a number by pacing out the penalty box.

From kick-off the fights began, just like in England. Costas made up for his crap ball skills by arguing with everybody. Eventually Angelos gave a penalty against us. The fair boy stepped up to take it. I knew what to do. I looked him in the eye. I saw how he was running and knew he would try to put it down my left, an easy save.

Angelos punched me on the arm. "You could be a good goalkeeper, Zeno. Let us practise every day. I like shooting, you like saving, we can both improve."

By this time it was getting hot, really, really hot. Everybody decided to go in the sea. I said I had no trunks but that didn't bother them. They just stripped off and jumped in. I sat on the side. Then we slid up a rocky path to some pine forests for some shelter. I realised it was lunchtime without me having thought about food all morning. That was a record.

Angelos got out the bread, halloumi and black olives and there was cold, sweet tea, in an old brandy bottle. He knocked open the tin that was full of strong tasting fish. I wouldn't eat them normally, but I was starving.

Vassos was moaning.

"Fanoulla, Fanoulla my love, my dream, when oh when will it be me. I want to be a man now, no more football and boys' games. I want to play with girls now."

"Do any girls play out?" I asked.

Angelos turned towards me. "And what are the games you would like to play with them? We know those games and that's why my sister is not allowed out."

It was Costas' turn to groan now.

"And what a sister! Her eyes so brown, her hair so fine..."

Angelos threw an olive at Costas. "Don't start getting any ideas about my sister."

He started to play fight Costas so he climbed up a tree to get out of Angelos way. He shouted:

"Felo mou, don't you want me as your brother-in-law?"

Angelos said to leave him up there. It was time to go for a snooze. As we walked back to the house Angelos said,

"The boys are the best eh? It is because we are one blood, always we will be friends."

I stopped and said in English.

"How are they the best? They are just like my friends in England. Why has everything to do with Cyprus have to be the best? And if you don't understand then you have to learn the best language. And it's not Greek."

CHAPTER NINETEEN

Over the next few weeks I got used to getting up early, feeding the chickens before collecting the eggs, otherwise if you tried collecting eggs before feeding them it was not only Slit Eye that would peck you but all the chickens. This morning I was awake before Angelos so it was my chance to wake him up with a punch in the stomach.

"So Zeno you have learnt to punch. You see the Cypriot way has made a man of you." He made to jiggle my belly, but I pushed him out of the way. "See you are not so fat now. Where is that stomach you had when you came first?"

Angelos went to the green shed so I got out the shiny trousers that Mum had got me for the journey from England. When I put them on it was like you could fit half of me again in the waist. I could do up the top button easily. And the other funny thing was they looked like they were too short.

"Coming down to the beach today Zeno? You are becoming a good swimmer like the turtles in Holy bay. Not like when you first came eh?"

I gave him a push. "If you learnt in the stinking baths at my school you would be a bad swimmer too. I love swimming in the beautiful sea."

Angelos poked my arm. "You are stronger too Zeno. Anyway today we might go and try and kill some ambelloboulla. Vassos has got a new catapult that he says will kill them even if they are flying high in the air, but you know Vassos:only he talks shit, shit and more shit. "

I shook my head. "Dad said he wanted to take me out to do something." He had said that we should go fishing but I'd been in one of the leaking fishing boats tied to the wooden pier and didn't want to go out to sea on anything like that.

"To go fishing you must go early in the morning Zeno. Before the sun gets high in the sky because then the fish can see you. No it won't be fishing he'll be taking you to."

I went downstairs as the grandmother was wrapping up some bread, boiled eggs, halloumi and olives in a tea towel and pouring some water into a bottle. She gave me some warm goat's milk to drink and one of her wide toothless smiles. I had even began to like the sharp taste of the goat's milk. And the holloumi was nothing like the ones we had at home. These were minty and dry.

Angelos came outside to join us. There was a question I had been meaning to ask him. Now looked like a good time.

"What happened to your Mum Angelos? Why do you live with your Grandmother?"

Angelos turned and faced me.

"Everybody knows but how could you? It is a simple story. My mother died giving me life. My family could not afford a doctor, there was one in the military base but Dad was a prisoner there so we couldn't get help. So grandmother tried but it was no good. I never knew my mother but everybody says she was a good woman."

I could see he was sad but I couldn't think of anything to say. I was saved by the rattle of Sotos' truck coming up the road.

Angelos went over to speak to his Dad so I slid between Dad and Sotos on a kind of box with a cushion on it, between the two other seats. I've never been inside the truck to see how Sotos was able to drive with his one hand.

He had a cushion behind him so that his big belly pushed onto the steering wheel. That way he could use his tummy to steer. The gear change was on the wheel so it wasn't far for him to move his good left hand.

The old truck took its time moving, the engine right in front of us loud and steamy. My feet were resting on what must have been the gearbox as I could hear grinding noises coming right underneath me and very soon it got so hot I had to put my feet up on the dashboard. Sotos drove really fast over the bumps, when we had to slow down like for a corner, the truck started jumping and rattling around as it hit the holes in the road. Then with a roar he accelerated hard. I couldn't understand how he could see where we were going because there was so much dust around. What if he hit something? But I thought he must be making so much noise that everybody could hear him coming from miles away.

Usually I would have been scared driving along like that. But I wasn't with Sotos. We leaned round a really tight corner and he gave me a smile. He had to shout above the engine noise.

"The truck is very good no? Zeno, what about helping me to drive eh? You're a clever boy you know what the gear lever does. When I tell you, push it up and if it's up, pull it down. Simple eh?"

Dad had let me turn the big white indicator switch towards me for left and away from me for right on the old Ford Prefect, but I'd never changed gears. I didn't know what they did really except they had something to do with going faster or slower.

He slowed down to go round a corner and shouted for me to push the lever up, but when I did the old truck crunched and shuddered as the lever got stuck in the middle of the column.

"You are too quick Zenoletti. Take your time; go easy, this is your friend, like between your legs eh? You must take it slow, show respect."

We got to a little bay by a shallow bit of the sea where we stopped. I could tell it was shallow because you could see the bottom of the water. I thought I was getting good at being a Cypriot.

Dad got out first and waved his arm around the bay.

"Here we are then Zeno: this beautiful place. What do you think of it?"

It didn't look too different from all the other bays around us except for a ruined church on the opposite side. There were lots of those everywhere too, but I could see this was a really big one with tall columns that were still standing. A huge bird came to look at us, squawking as it flew up from the church.

Sotos stood on some big rocks.

"We will have to do something about these stones on the beach Manoli."

Dad said he would build the new house with a window looking straight out on the beach so he could see everybody take a swim.

What new house did Dad mean? Then I remembered the talk in the Kefenieon that first day. Was Dad planning to buy a house in Cyprus?

Sotos walked back to the truck. He always put a tray underneath the engine to collect any oil that leaked out. Dad was standing by himself looking at a fishing boat that was putt-putting its way back towards the village.

He threw his arms out wide and took a big breath in.

"Son, look around you, feel the sun on your face and smell this beautiful air. I want you to have a new life, away from those English people that hurt you and spit at us and call us names. I want us to be a family again, with our own people that speak our own language and have the same blood. This is going to be your new home. Here I will build a beautiful hotel." He was scrunching his eyes looking over the bay. It was the longest he had ever spoken to me, ever. Usually we were interrupted by Mum or by something happening.

"We will get the insurance money. Then we can sell the café. We can all come back to Cyprus, to this beautiful place. Your Mother will be happier here with her own friends, Maria could come and open a hairdressing shop and we would find her a good husband, a good Cypriot boy. Pedri can play some music, Dinos is good with money, he can see to the books."

He stopped to look at me.

"And you Zeno mou. I can see you are good in the kitchen, You have the most important thing that good cooks need, taste and smell. You can help me cook and then when you are ready, take over from me."

He walked away from me pacing along the beach, counting out loud talking to himself. He said Stomei will organise everything, he just needed the insurance money to come through.

Sotos had come back down now with some paper. He sat with Dad and started drawing and measuring things. He pointed at a line where he said the road would be and that's where all the customers would come.

I climbed over the rocks until I got to the top of the hill. The big bird had circled overhead, looked at us and was now swooping back down into the centre of the church, maybe he had a nest there or something. I looked out over the bay at the fishing boat still making its slow way back to the village, its brown sides contrasting with the blue of the sea. All around were rocks, scattered on the sandy beach. Then I realised. I wanted to see a proper street with street lights, or houses with proper gardens and hedges. Why did none of the roads have pavements? You had to get out of the way of any traffic that went past, usually into a scratchy bush that always seemed to grow by the side of the road.

Working in a kitchen? Why did Dad think I liked working in the kitchen? It was dirty and messy. I liked eating the food but being a cook? I knew I couldn't be a footballer like my friends or a train driver because all that steam made me cough, but a cook? No thanks.

The truck wheezed into life and Sotos drove off leaving Dad by himself. I scrambled down the hill hitting my big toe on a half buried rock. I didn't have to think about what to say. It all came out in a rush.

"Look Dad you've got to listen. Dad I like it here and everything, the football, sea, Angelos and Vassos and Costas too. But it's not my home. Nobody wants to come, especially me. Mum hates all the village people. Maria hates goat shit. Pedri is not interested in no bouzouki band and Dinos is only interested in his job and doing that ban the bomb stuff. And I won't come here. It stinks, it's too hot and I want my friends. And I hate cooking."

For once he didn't do that Dad not really looking at you thing that he did. He went to speak, stopped, opened his mouth to say something and stopped again.

He said, "Not like cooking? But you always helped me squeeze the lemons for soupan. Or roll the meatballs for the koftas? Why wouldn't you want to be a cook? Like me. Or stay here with your new friends?"

Dad looked surprised when I pushed him.

"I don't want any Cypriot friends. You were never interested in my English friends and now all you want to do is give me Cyprus ones. I want my home. Not this dump."

It was like Dad didn't know what to do.

"You never take me anywhere. Dave's Dad takes him to the Spurs and fishing and stuff and lets him go on his scooter. All you do is make me squeeze lemons. You never get me books that I like, only crap Greek ones. Michael's Dad gets him his favourite comics. You don't even know what comics I like." I walked off towards the ruins of the church.

I hadn't gone very far when I heard the truck returning. Sotos parked up and called to us that he had work to do. He said we would need our own car. A cousin of his had a Morris Minor that he could sell us, very good, very cheap. Dad started to walk up towards Sotos. I followed. It felt like the sandy beach was alive, pushing against me as I tried to get to the truck.

I was glad of the noise of the engine as we drove back. Sotos and Dad were still talking business so they dropped me at the house. Dad said to come to the kafenenion later so we could talk. I needed to go into the stupid shed so I didn't argue. The stink of animal shit was everywhere, it was really hot and the midges were buzzing really loud today. I noticed the crumbling walls of the house, the cracked windows, the rickety furniture held together with other bits of wood. If we stayed in Cyprus how long would we be living in this dump?

I thought I'd go upstairs to the bedroom, but it was too hot to stay in and too hot to stay out. The only thing to do was to go down to the beach. I had to find a way of telling Maria of Dad's plans. She could change things if anybody could.

My toe was hurting from hitting it on the rock, I'd left the bundle of food in Sotos' truck so I grabbed a bit of stale bread that was at the house and drunk some lemon water that the old women kept in a glass jug that she said her daughter had got her from England. Underneath it had 'Made in Great Britain' stamped on it and for some reason that made me want to cry.

I took the short cut through the dried stream, climbing over the fallen tree. I remembered Mum's warning and watched out for any snakes that might be around. I never got to see any so I didn't know why Mum was so bothered. The trick was to make lots of noise as you walked along. Snakes didn't like you creeping up on them. I made lots of noise anyway. Costas said I would be very thin if I had to hunt for a living as all the animals would have run for miles before I got to them.

The boys were playing stonies, someone made a tall pile of stones one on top of the other and each took it in turns to pull a stone out of the pile. The person who pulled the stone that made the pile fall down had to do something bad, like climb a tree; or run to the sea without your shorts on. Stupid stuff like that.

"Hey Zeno, you are just in time. We are going to try out Vassos' machine. We can get some birds so we can eat them for our supper tonight."

"I'm sick of your stupid Greek games." I said. "I don't want to kill no birds. What have they ever done to you? And anyway, they taste of nothing. They're all bones when you eat them. Leave the poor birds alone."

"Hey we said no English anymore. Why you speaking English again? Your Greek was getting really good and your skin is brown and you are not so fat. You're becoming a real Greek boy. Don't start being an English malaga again."

"It is my language. I don't want to speak no Greek. I don't want to stay in this poxy country. Dad says that we are going to stay here, but he's wrong. There's no way I can stay here." I told them about Dad's plans and they laughed because they were all planning to go to England.

"There will only be you and Vassos left because all of us will be in England," Costas said.

My foot was really hurting now, my feet burnt from the sand. I had skinned my knee taking the short cut, blood was dripping down my leg and the flies were buzzing around the cut. I had been really hungry, but now my stomach felt like there was no room for food.

I walked up the hill not knowing where to go and took the path between a church that the Turks used, or used to. This one wasn't crumbling, just smashed up and empty. A sharp stomach turning smell warned me as I turned a corner that the goats were using the path too. The leader of the pack looked up with those scary eyes, but even he could see I wasn't going to be messed with today. I knew what to do. Vassos was a goat herd and he said you had to go straight towards a goat pack, shouting and waving your arms. Throwing rocks was good too. They can't see that there is only one of you, Vassos had explained. So they get out of your way. He said to be careful though, they always come back for more.

I took a deep breath, picked up some stones and gave the goats a few North London swear words. The goats were not used to crazy English people and took a step back. Luckily I was nearly at the end of the path. I couldn't turn my back on them. That's when they would come at you.

I recognised a house and remembered that Stomei lived there. I wanted a drink, maybe he would have an idea of contacting England? I went and knocked on his door.

Stomei came to the door looking a bit wobbly. I could smell the sharp aniseed smell of raki.

"Ha! It is Zeno. Have you come to play chess my boy? You are a very clever boy. Come in come in. You have left those bad boys behind eh? Those boys that made fun of you? Come. I am having a little drink. You should have a little. Just between men eh?"

Something made me wait on the doorstep. As he disappeared inside I went to leave. But my foot hurt and my mouth was dry. He shouted out for me to come in. I thought I was being silly. I may as well go in.

Stomei's house was stuffed full of toys and games. A huge jigsaw of London was set on the floor. I recognized Tower Bridge and The Houses of Parliament. Stomei pointed at the sofa.

"Sit, sit. You like my house eh? It is a good place for boys to come and play."

He passed me a drink. I just wanted water. I recognized the smell of raki.

"Here is your drink. Ahh, I have spilt some on your shorts. Stupid me, here let me dry them. Take them off, take them off and I will dry them." I didn't want to take my shorts off though. Stomei went into the kitchen to get a cloth.

"Now let me wipe you. Just there. Just there. Is that nice? I see you're a big boy for your age. Soon you will be a grown man. Have you seen what a grown man looks like? Here look, look."

Stomei started to fiddle with his trousers. Breathing heavily he moved towards me.

"Just your hand. Just touch. Touch."

Pushing him away I kicked over the jigsaw and headed for the door.

He shouted after me.

"No don't run away. I will not hurt you. It's just a bit of fun. Our secret hey? Look don't be upset, take, take this. Take it. Two shillings. Keep quiet eh? It's our secret. You mustn't tell anybody otherwise you'll be in trouble. Nobody must know, do you understand? Okay just go. Go. I am disappointed in you Zeno. I thought we would be friends. Now you have nobody."

As I ran out of his house I could see the British Army base at the top of the hill. Maybe I will be safe there. I cut through, past a scrubby bush, onto a black tarmac road. And a pavement! A proper English one with a curb and everything. I walked up to two soldiers guarding the entrance. The one nearest to me had that skinny spotty look, like one of the Teddy boys that had burnt down the cafe. The other was red faced with ginger hair. You could see he was too hot, his face dripped with sweat. They were both standing to attention, holding guns that were resting on their shoulders.

Before I could say anything the ginger one said out of the corner of his mouth, "Fuck off gyppo, before I put this bayonet somewhere you won't like."

I started to say that I was English like them. But I was so used to speaking in Greek that I forgot to speak English.

"What's the little fuck saying Harry?"

"Fucked if I know Sid, but I'm sure it's not good. Allay allay just fuck off, capish?"

The ginger one turned and pointed his gun towards me. I was so scared that I couldn't move. Or talk. All I could think of was how I would manage with one arm like Sotos. I was saved by a motorbike that came roaring out of the base. The rider saw me and stopped to speak to the two soldiers, gave them some cigarettes while smiling and shaking their hands. He got me to sit in front of him because the back of the bike had some boxes strapped on the seat.

It was Yiannis from that first night. "What are you doing here son of Manoli? Keep away from this scum, they will shoot you and bury you without anybody knowing. I laugh and joke with them to take their money, but you keep away, eh?

I held tight to the handlebars as we bumped our way back to the village. The bike bounced and rattled so much that the boxes fell off the back of the bike. They crashed open and four long guns fell on the ground. Yiannis stopped to pick them up. He put his fingers to his lips.

"Say nothing eh? Nothing, understand?

CHAPTER TWENTY

I found a shady olive tree up in the hills with a smooth stone underneath. Most days now I came up to the hills. After that time on the beach Dad kept away from me, hurrying out after breakfast and not coming back until late. Also I had enough of the boys. Angelos tried to get me to come out again and when he saw I was serious about not going he showed me some English books left behind when his cousin went to England. Classic books by Charles Dickens and William Shakespeare, but also some Sherlock Holmes that I had read before. I couldn't understand Shakespeare so I tried Dickens: 'It was the best of times; it was the worst of times,' but I got all the different names muddled up, so I decided I would prefer reading Sherlock Holmes.

I stretched out my legs along the warm rock and felt the sun on my face under the old hat of Sotos I wore to keep the flies away. I had some juicy figs wrapped up ready to eat, but that would bring the flies over, so I left them for later. I could feel my dick getting hard again. It felt like it got hard all the time now, but I didn't want to be like Vassos and keep rubbing myself off every ten minutes. I better try to concentrate on the book.

It was funny to be reading about life in old England while I was sitting in the heat of Cyprus.

In the distance I could hear the goats making their way down the other side of the hill, their bells clanking so everybody knew exactly where they were. I wasn't afraid of them anymore. It was like they knew I wasn't scared so they didn't bother me now. They were being followed by a boy, Salim. He was Turkish. The other boys had pointed him out to me. I saw him looking at me so I waved. He waved back. We looked at each other for a bit and then he came walking towards me, the goats following.

"Gia sou. I am Salim. Why are you not with the other boys?"

I said "How come you speak good English?"

He looked around him before replying.

"It is why the other boys don't like me. My father is English, a soldier and my mother is Turkish. I only speak a little Greek."

I told him that they had kept away from me after I stopped speaking Greek to them. He nodded and pointed at my book.

"You are reading Sherlock Holmes? I like him too. My father sends me some of his books. Soon I will be in England and it helps me know what it is like."

"What? Sherlock Holmes is nothing like England now. Nobody runs after plaster Napoleons saying 'By Jove' and 'I am exceedingly grateful'. Anyway the bad people are always foreigners, like this one, Beppo. You will be a foreigner in England too."

"But it is the same here. Everybody tells me I am bad because my father is English and my mother Turkish."

"And that's what the English tell me. That's why my Dad wants to bring me back here."

Salim stood up.

"But my Dad says it will be good in England when he sends for me, maybe this year, maybe soon. I have to go now. I have some books that you might like. What about Treasure Island? Or some H.G Wells books? I also have Animal Farm. That is very good. Come tomorrow and I will bring them."

The next few days I met Salim and I tried to tell him about England, the rain, Hancock's half hour and football matches. He said his father supported Leyton Orient so I told him they were shit and only Tottenham were the team to support. Salim said he would write to his Dad about supporting both teams and I explained you can't do that. It has to be one or the other.

He often brought some nice fresh haloumi and warm bread from his Mum. This lunchtime we were sitting eating some vine leaves stuffed with rice and nuts, when someone shouted my name. Looking down I could see Vassos and Costas at the bottom of the hill.

Costas shouted. "Zeno, you have gone away from us but are playing with the Turk boy? Come away now. Or we will make this boy go. It is the only way with dirty Turks."

They started to scramble up the hill towards us so I expected Salim to beat it out of there. Instead he pushed me behind him.

He turned to me and said.

"Leave these boys to me. My father has

taught me how to fight. I am not scared."

After a lot of puffing because the hill was steep, the boys arrived in front of Salim and me.

Costas said "Zeno come and stand with us. We are your blood. We will not hurt this boy. Turks always run away anyway."

I knew what I had to do. I pointed at Costas.

"Leave Salim alone. He's not done you any harm. Just because he is not Greek you beat him up. I get beat up in England just because I'm not English. If you beat him up you will have to fight me too. And you showed me how to punch."

The boys looked at Salim and then at me. Although Salim was small you could see he was tough. He had his fists bunched and ready. Shaking his head Costas turned to Vassos.

"It is bad Vassos. Bad that one of our own has become a Turk lover. If you fight us you can never come back Zeno. You have made your choice."

Costas spat on the ground at Salim's feet, the sign that he wanted to fight. Salim took a step forward and went to throw a punch at Costas. He missed so Costas managed to hit Salim with a fist in the stomach. Vassos and me didn't know what to do. We liked each other so why would we fight? By now Costas and Salim had fallen to the floor and were rolling around in the dust. I wanted to help Salim but he didn't look like he was losing the fight. Vassos and me had the same idea at the same time. Both of us grabbed the boys to stop them fighting. Someone punched me in the face, it might have been Salim but we managed to pull them off each other.

I got in front of Salim and Vassos held Costas back.

Costas shouted, "Leave me, I was winning, he was finished."

Salim replied with his Greek swear words. It was going to be hard to stop them fighting again. Then the sound of a truck grinding up the hill stopped us. We could see it was Sotos's truck. It stopped in the road below. Angelos jumped out and waved at me to come down from the hill. I could see by the look on his face that it was serious.

Angelos shouted "Zeno, your father has some bad news from England. You must come with us. Now! Amesos. And boys what are you doing here? Stop fighting and come down now."

CHAPTER TWENTY ONE

Me, Vassos and Costas jumped into the truck after I checked Salim was alright. Blood was dripping down from a cut on my lip so I used one of the rags on the floor of the truck to wipe my mouth. It didn't take long to get to the village. As we parked up we could see Dad standing by the water fountain talking with some men I hadn't seen before. He was wearing a jacket, shirt and tie. It had to be serious.

With one hand on the side, I swivelled round from the front of the truck to land facing backwards, just like Angelos showed me. I always thought it looked cool and here I was doing it.

As I walked towards Dad I heard a shout. The blond Manchester United fan cycled straight towards me shouting. "Turkish lover, Turkish lover." He had got hold of an old green ex-Army bike that was too big for him. The only way he could stop was by jumping off. I did a nifty little side step just at the last minute, pushed him as he went by and left him sprawling on the floor.

Dad saw what happened and came over to help the boy get up. He turned to me while he was brushing the dust off the boy's clothes.

"Zeno, why do you hurt your friends, when he was just having fun?"

I pushed Dad. The second time in a few days.

"Dad, I keep telling you they are not my friends. Just leave me alone."

I walked away not knowing which way to go. Angelos ran up to me. He put his hand on my shoulder.

"You are right Zeno; this is not your country. It is good that you fight for what you want. That means you are a lion not a pussycat. You are leaving here very soon and I may never see you again. Let's be friends before you leave."

I shook my head. "What do you mean leave? What do you know about me leaving?"

"This is what happens if you go the mountains with your old books. You don't know the news. Your father got a phone call in the office at the town hall from your brother in England. There is something wrong with the insurance and you need to go back. Your father has been trying to get tickets and has found some. Tomorrow you go back to England. Tonight is your last night in Cyprus."

CHAPTER TWENTY TWO

I decided to go the long way round back to the house, past the nice beach. Maybe it would be the last time I would see it?

A voice called out. It was Costas, sitting with Vassos.

"English, come let's be friends again. This is your last night. Let us make it special."

I knew what I needed to say.

"I want to say goodbye to you all. But do not call me English. I am Zeno. That is my name. Not English or greebo or bubble or grease-ball. Zeno. OK?"

"Ok Eng...Zeno. Let us start by drinking. My father has given me some wine for tonight."

The only wine I liked was the sweet Cyprus wine that the priests used to give you, the others made me feel sick but I wasn't going to let that stop me tonight. We met up with Angelos and he opened the old whisky bottle to pass the wine round. It tasted OK, thicker than some of the other stuff I'd had.

"What are we going to do, to make this nice night special?" Vassos asked.

Angelos took a long swig out of the whisky jar.

"There is only one thing that a ten-year-old boy needs on his final night in Cyprus." They both looked at each other and laughed. Angelos passed the bottle to me.

"But I need to know Zeno. Why do you like England so much? I am going there soon to be with my uncle. Tell us what it is like."

It was a good question. I knew I wanted to be there but why?

"Well my sister is there and my friends and I like the T.V, Fireball XL5 and Hancock's Half Hour and I like *'Just William'* books about village fetes and going to see his father in the study and poetry and the way Pretty Boy Harry makes fun of Rudyard as 'ruddy hard' and I like school dinners and rain and upstairs on the bus when it's a cold day and how people say please and excuse me, nobody says that here and—"

"Stop now Zeno," Angelos held up a hand. "I don't understand. But tell me there must be some things you like here in Cyprus?"

"Oh yes, I like how tomatoes taste when they are picked straight from the bush or how fish smell so fresh from the sea and how everybody is the same. There's no top-boys or high up, everybody has the piss taken out of them. But nothing works, the electric goes out, there's no pavements, no T.V—"

"No more Zeno, let us show you something that is the best, eh? Something you won't be able to see in your precious England. Vassos let's go now. You know where."

We went along the beach to the old Turkish part of the town. One house stood out as being neat and tidy and still lived in. As we went closer Vassos starting groaning again. We stopped when we saw someone in the front room. It was Fanoulla. This had to be her house. There was another groan from Vassos.

"Let's hide and maybe we can see her undressing."

Angelos held up the wine bottle. "No more hiding. This is what little boys do. Soon we won't need to spy on women undressing. We will have our own ones. Fanoulla wants to see you Zeno. She asked me to bring you before you go back. She is expecting you. You are a lucky boy. Once you have finished come down to my father's house. He is doing a whole lamb on the barbecue, fresh from the mountains. It will be delicious: something you don't have in England."

Laughing they pushed me towards the tiled wall of the small house, the entrance full of sweet smelling pots of flowers. Before I could knock, the door had opened and Fanoulla stood tall in front of me, wearing a cool looking white dress.

She smiled.

"Good. You have come. You are welcome. Come in." Waving at the boys she told them to go away. "You can come and spy at my window when I am undressing another time. Not now."

Her house was full of old looking statues and swirly cloths hanging from the ceiling. She told me to sit on a plump cushion while she got some drinks. My head felt heavy. What was going to happen with her? Of all the boys why had she chosen me? Soon she was back with tea that had mint in it and some sweet baklavas. As she bent forward to put the drink down she saw me staring at her bosoms.

"Now don't start getting any ideas little man. You men have the same thought about women but it is too soon for you to become stupid with that madness. You have a little time yet. I have asked you here to tell you about Zeno. Your Uncle. What do you know about him?"

I wasn't sure if I heard right.

"My Uncle? I have an uncle called Zeno?

Fanoulla shook her head.

"Had an Uncle. He died more than twenty years ago. Your mother's older brother. I am not surprised she does not talk of him. Nobody does. He was as good as he needed to be. Him and me, well we were both young and foolish. He did some bad things. The girls kept away. Or else. He was his Mother's, your grandmother's, God rest her the old witch, well, her favourite. You can guess what she thought of me and her darling son being together. Anyway you were named after him. The last wish of the old witch."

"But what happened. Why doesn't anybody talk about him?"

Fanoulla stood up, pulled her wrap around her and went over to a bright purple coloured carved wooden sideboard. Opening a shiny box she took out a coloured cigarette and lit it with a hissing, silver lighter.

"It was your Mother's fault. That's why she doesn't come back anymore. Or didn't. All is forgotten now. Your Mother was small but she knew she should not have been playing near the British bases. Zeno was sent to get her. She was stuck up a tree because she had seen some snakes. She never liked snakes."

"That's what she kept saying to me. Always be careful of snakes!"

"They won't hurt you. But she was always one to make fussarria, always crying and complaining. He got her down from the tree, then she remembered that he said that he had some business to sort out and sent her home. The next thing, yes the next thing...."

Fanoulla stopped to take a drink of the sweet tea. There must have been ten sugars in the mixture as mint tea that I had tasted before had been really bitter.

"Well the next thing is that they found his body two days later. A bullet through his heart. Probably a British soldier got scared and panicked. In those days we couldn't say anything. Just bring him home and bury him. I know we could not have been together but to lose him that way....."

"What about me though? Why was I called after him?"

"Your grandmother. She was dying and said that unless your mother's next son was called Zeno she would put a curse on the family. Nobody could risk that from her. Now you know everything. Take some baklava. They are from another Zeno, the baker. The best."

I remembered what Dad had said as we got off the boat. That we would be safe in Cyprus. So far I had a gun pointed at me, I've been beaten up by my so called blood brothers, chased by goats, attacked by Turks and then had to learn to avoid poisonous snakes and mad chickens. Not to mention that creep Stomei. Now I find out that I am named after a dead uncle because of a curse from a witch of a grandmother. In England I only had Baz and homework to worry about. I couldn't wait to get back.

CHAPTER TWENTY THREE

I started feeling ill at Sotos' farewell barbecue but I put that down to some dodgy meat. My face began to swell up on the boat to Italy. I saw the ship's doctor who said the cut from the fight with Costas had got infected probably from that old rag I wiped my mouth with in Sotos' van. There were some Mums on board who looked after me, rubbing garlic and fresh onion on the wound. I spent most of the trip sleeping. I was all right by the time we got to the ferry to England except then I was seasick again as the crossing was so rough.

Dad didn't get a taxi from the station this time, just a crowded Piccadilly Line tube and then an even more crowded 243 bus from the station. We managed to get the suitcases into the cubbyhole next to the conductor.

"Straight off the boat are you?" he said.

Dad had packed the suitcases with halloumi and olive oil so my hands were stinging as I tried to carry the suitcase in one hand and keep my blue trousers from falling down with the other. As we walked towards the café we could see it had been freshly boarded up and painted.

Dad said, "How much has that cost me?"

I got to the side door first and opening it shouted, "Hullo anybody home?" I hoped Maria would answer but the first thing we noticed as we walked through the door was the pile of boxes in the corridor. The door to the front room opened, I thought it might be Mum, but it was Mavis with bright red lipstick painted on her face, waving her hands in the air like she was trying to cool them down.

"Hello Mr Antonio and hello Zeno love, you back? You've caught us girls together. Your misses is having one of her parties, it's really exciting. Do you want to see my new nail varnish?"

We went into the kitchen, leaving the suitcases in the hall, I wasn't going to carry them any further. Mavis shouted to Mum that the men were back. Mum came out to the kitchen only it didn't look like Mum. She wasn't wearing black anymore. She had on a flowery kind of top and a red skirt. I could see she had something on her face, like lipstick. Her hair seemed different too.

"Oh you are back early, look at you, Zeno mou, you have grown up in so few weeks." Then in English she said: "I must get back to the party, it will be finished soon and then we can speak." Mum went back into the front room and told everybody to leave. There must have been ten or so women. I recognised some of them from the café.

Mum came into the kitchen once all the women had left and gave me a hug.

"What's with the new clothes Mum?" I asked.

Mum went to open a box as we spoke, full of bright women's clothes.

"Well Zeno I couldn't sell clothes when I

looked like I am going to a, what's it called in English? Ah yes a funeral. But look at you Zeno. You've lost weight and grown up. You must tell me everything. And in English: I want to speak only English now."

I started to tell her about the heat and the flies and I was about to tell her Dad's plans when he came in from looking at the café downstairs.

"Who are these women and what are they doing in the house? And why are you wasting time having a party in the afternoon when there is so much to do?"

Mum picked up some clothes from the box.

"Wasting time is what's putting food on the table. I'm selling the perfume and clothes I get from Evangellia in the market and Maria knows someone who has handbags so there is everything here for the women. I am making good money, easy money that doesn't mean chopping and frying and washing up. You just get things in the box, take them out of the box and you sell them for a profit, clean easy money. It is what the women want. And I can make £20 a day without having to stink of fat and grease."

"No you just stink of perfume and face powder. You look like a pudana at Kiki's Kafeneio. Even you are forgetting our lives and where we came from but not me. Now let's have some food and we can talk. Dinos will be here soon with this letter. What is there for dinner? "

"I didn't know what time you would be back and anyway we were busy. Me and Maria haven't been cooking much when it is just us to eat. We found something really good. A Chinese place where they put food in boxes to bring home, a whole dinner for just a few shillings, everything, meat, rice, soup. And all you have to do is wash up the plates. Maria is bringing some when she comes home."

"Food from China?" Dad said. "What are we eating frogs legs and mitzoles that sting you? Are you serious? I will have some halloumi and olives that I have bought back from Cyprus. Keep your stinking food."

Same old, same old, I thought. I went upstairs for a lie down. I squeezed past Pedri's bed, Mum still kept it made up for him. No more, I said it to myself. And then again out loud. Picking up Pedri's mattress I tipped it over. I was surprised by my strength. The bed underneath had a metal frame painted blue with springs covered by a wire mesh. I picked that up too, the frame crashing on the floor as I overturned it. Mum and Dad stopped arguing, Mum shouted up to me to ask me what was I doing? I went out of the room to shout back.

"I don't want Pedri's bed here; it takes up all the room. He's not coming home. And I want my own room."

Before Mum's expected explosion, the front door opened downstairs: Dinos and Maria! I ran downstairs to see them. They were carrying some paper bags that smelt delicious.

Maria gave me a hug, but I was nearly as tall as her now. She was fussing over me telling me how slim I looked. Dad pushed by.

"Dinos, the letter. Let me see the letter."

Dinos took it from his jacket.

"Look it says it here, in black and white, no messing." Dinos read from the letter, "Due to non-payment of premiums for the prescribed period, which comprises a full twelve months prior to any claims, we regretfully inform you that it is not possible to meet this claim in this instance."

Dad snatched the letter from Dinos and read it for himself.

"Those bastards can't get away with this. I missed a few payments when things were bad, but I was catching up. We have to do something. I will get Fodos' son to look at this, he is a solicitor. I will ring him now."

Dinos laughed. "He's an estate agent Dad, he does some house buying. Let's face it we are stuffed: big time. Anyway let's eat while it's hot. Chicken chow mein my favourite. Zeno, or should I call you Mr. Zeno you've grown up so much, how was Cyprus? And well done on your school results."

Mum followed Dad out to the phone downstairs so there was just me, Dinos and sis. The smell of the food as the boxes were opened made me realise how hungry I was so I wasn't paying much attention to Dinos.

"Zeno. Your school results. Didn't Dad tell you?"

"Tell me what Den?"

"What? He didn't say? I told him when I rang Cyprus. You've only gone and got into all the top sets for next year. Even for maths, Gawd knows how you did that. Or how I did that as it's me you have to thank for that result."

I still didn't understand "So that's good is it

Dinos?"

"Good? It means you are in the 11 plus set, they expect you to pass and that means the grammar school. It's brilliant , not good."

Maria handed me some bony meat dripping with sauce.

"Well done Zeno, here try your first barbecue spare rib." They were delicious. And then some juicy chicken in a nice sauce and spaghetti like things called chop suey, fried with lots of vegetables.

Maria was using stick things to eat with, or trying to.

"So what happened Zeno? Lots of goat shit was there?"

That's when I told them. About Dad's plan. The hotel, Dinos could do the books. Maria could run a hair dressing business. And I would cook.

They laughed. Dinos said "It's the same old same same old. We are going back, everything will be great, blah blah."

I finished the last of the chicken, it left a strange buzzing taste in my mouth and a tingling in my fingers and toes.

"Thing is Den, it was worse than here. There were guns and people being killed and I found out about Uncle Zeno.

Dinos and Maria looked at each other.

Maria said "Oh that old thing. Don't bother about stupid old stories like that. And don't talk to Mum about it. She gets upset."

Then I remembered. That Maria might get upset if I told her that I had seen her with Steve? Maybe there was no point in saying anything.

Maria would be getting married soon anyway. To a nice Greek boy. I needed to sort out my love life as well. When will I be seeing Zash again?

CHAPTER TWENTY-FOUR

Dave kicked a stone that went skidding across the road.

"So what was it like, Zen?"

"I loved it. The spare ribs were so juicy and sticky, with a lovely sweet taste. The only thing I didn't like was these watery things that were called bean-sprouts that didn't really taste of anything."

"No I'm not talking about your Chinese takeaway you wally." I'd knocked for Dave on the way to school: our first day back.

"I'm talking about your trip: back to the bleeding home country and all that bollocks. That's what my Mum makes us do most years. Staying in a stinking farm in the middle of nowhere smelling cow-shit all day and nothing to do but chuck stones at the rabbits. Even in the middle of summer, all it does is rain. You can never get warm."

"Cyprus is just the same except it's too hot. And you smell goat-shit instead of cow-shit. Anyway my Dad has this crazy idea of us going back there."

"What do you mean Zen? What would you go back for?"

"Something about building a hotel and all of us going to work in it. You should have heard what my Mum said. Funny thing is: all the Cypriot boys want to do is come here."

"That's what my Mum says about the Irish. They all want to come over here. She says she would have a house full of relatives if she wasn't careful." Dave's face lit up. "Zen, Michael's Dad said Welsh Davies has got arrested: something about fiddling with a minor. He's gone. That fucker's gone. No more stripping bollock naked for him. Let's see what the new P.E. teacher is like though. They're all perves if you ask me."

We started jumping up and down shouting out, "Davies has gone! Davies has gone!" as we walked towards the rec. Turning the corner we saw a man standing by the gates, dressed up in Teddy boy cloths, tight trousers and black jacket.

He turned towards us. "That pouf Davies has gone boys, but you two girls are still here. And so am I." It was Baz! "That's not different. I'm not at baby school anymore. Moved on to better things. But I still need some dosh, spondoolicks, cash-in-hand. Got the message? You know the score dickheads. So for the time being: au revoir, as they say on the continent. Business as usual eh?" So Baz wasn't going away.

As we walked away from him I knew I had to do something different this year. What would the boys on the beach do?

"I am not getting fucked over by that bastard this year, Dave. Telling you straight: he is bad news, I know. Now tell me where Zash is. Have you seen her by the rec?"

Dave stopped.

"Mate I've got some more bad news. I meant

to tell you before. It's Zash. They came back while you were away. Her Dad got some job in the government or something. They've gone back, gone back to Bongo, Bongo land. Gone for good."

I couldn't think straight as we went into my first lesson, English. Not mixed ability anymore, I was in the top set, not with the dickheads. But I wasn't with Zash. Or Dave. But Seamus was there. He can't be happy at that. A top boy can't be seen to being clever.

A new English teacher, one of those little wiry guys with a half beard round his sticky-out chin, introduced himself. Mr Sellers, Peter Sellers. "But no, I am not the famous one: ha, ha," he said.

"Now boys and girls I want you to write. Really write. Don't worry about spelling or grammar. Express yourselves. That's all that matters. Now what about that famous first exercise after holidays. Write about what you did. Where did you go if anywhere? Sights and sounds. Just write freely."

Where to start? The heat? The smells? Dad's crazy plan? And now, Zash not being here. So then I just wrote it as it happened: the journey. What it felt like to drive up into the mountains. Playing with the boys on the beach. The soldiers I saw at the base that night. I was writing page after page. I knew my writing was getting messier to the point where no one else could read it. I didn't care. I just needed to get it all down. Even when Mr Sellers told us to stop, I couldn't. I just carried on writing. I wanted to get to the end when we got back to England. He said I could stay in the classroom during break times if I wanted to, just hand it to him when I was finished, but I couldn't do that. That would be what the swots would do.

Next was P.E. Let's see if Dave was right and P.E. teachers are all the same. This one was called Burgess, Richard Burgess. Straight off Pretty Boy tried it on. "Mr Burgess, can we call you Dick for short? We called our last P.E. teacher Dick too, even though that wasn't his name."

Mr Burgess looked at Pretty Boy.

"Maybe Mr Wilson, would care to run three times round the pitch for being a smart Alec." First round to Mr Burgess. As Pretty Boy run round the pitch as slow as he could, Mr Burgess gave us a speech.

"Firstly Mr Davies has gone. His was the old style view of P.E. For me sports shouldn't be about punishment, this was not wartime anymore. Unless you mess around like Mr Wilson here, sport is about enjoyment and reaching your potential. There won't be any favourites. There won't be any winners and losers. We are all going to join in. Now let's start by boys' footie. We all like that."

Instead of the top boys choosing, he picked football teams by going around the group naming people A and B. All the A's were in one team and all he B's in the other. No picking.

As Pretty Boy finally finished, Mr Burgess said that seeing as he ran so slowly he had better get fit by doing a few more circuits, unless he did the next one quicker. Pretty Boy picked up the pace then.

I was in the best team with Pretty Boy,

Harry, Winston and Dave on the wing. Before anybody said, I told Pretty Boy that I wanted to go in goal. It was my position. I'd had plenty of practice on the Cyprus beaches. I paced out the pitch like Zash told me. Then stretching exercises just for show. After a few minutes the ball came to one of our defenders; I came out of the goal and I told him to pass it back. Take control of your area. I crouched down when the ball came towards me, gathered it in my arms and made sure it came into my stomach so that there wasn't any chance of it bouncing away. I picked up the ball, bounced it once, then bounced again and keeping my eye on the middle of the ball, I gave it a good thwack to reach the halfway line. Pretty Boy Harry was quick, the ball bounced over one of their defenders into his path, he took a shot and scored a great goal. As he came running back, he gave me the thumbs up.

Nothing was going to get past me, I could feel that the ball was glued to my hands and we finished at half time two nil up. This didn't please Seamus who was on the other side. He wasn't used to losing.

As we changed over at half time he scowled at me.

"Look grease-ball, you've maybe lost a bit of weight, but remember if I'm shooting I'm scoring understand?" I already had Baz on my back, but I didn't want Seamus pushing me around too.

The second half was different. They were playing better and they scored one early on. And then they scored another: two-two. A few minutes to go and Seamus was put through. It's like our defenders stood there as he ran towards goal: just me and him. It wouldn't have been any shame to let him score, but I wasn't about to. He came towards me; I waited until the right time, rushed him and made a lunge for the ball. As I got the ball, he fell over, cracking his face on the still hard ground.

Everybody stopped. Mr Sellers came over and asked him if he was all right. Seamus got groggily up and said he didn't want the rest, that he knew someone that might be needing one soon. He looked over to me.

I kept out of Seamus' way at lunch time, but I knew I had to find a chance to show Seamus that I wasn't scared. Just before the whistle went Deano our new form master called me over.

"This letter has been left for you by the clever coloured girl, whatever her name was. I was asked to give it to you and I am discharging my duty. Don't be late for registration. I am running a tight ship this year."

He handed me a letter written in that blue thin paper that Mum sometimes got from Cyprus. Air mail. I opened it carefully. I recognised Zash's neat small writing.

"Dear Zeno. I am sorry I have been taken away from England but Dad got the offer of a good job and we decided to all go back. I really liked you Zeno and will always remember the nice times we had. I hope you had a nice time in Cyprus. I love it here but still miss England. I will write you again when we get a proper address. Keep practising the goalkeeping and maybe you could write your news when you can. Besties

Zash x."

She finished with a kiss. I knew that was what that x meant.

The bell went so I walked into registration thinking about the letter. As I walked in I saw that someone had drawn a huge dick on the blackboard. It would be Seamus. We all knew it was him including Deano. But when he asked who had given us the pleasure of their anatomical knowledge everybody kept quiet, except me. I had a plan. This was my chance to show Seamus that I was on his side now. I put my hand up. Seamus glared at me.

"It was me Sir. Me. I did it."

"Well I'm disappointed in you Mr Antonio," Deano said. "I thought you would be using your undoubted talents in other directions, but maybe a discussion with the deputy headmaster will convince you of the error of this new direction that you are embarking on."

I knew what a discussion with the "killer major" McGregor meant: the Cane. He was well-known for it. That was his job. 'Major R.B. McGregor, D.S.O, M.C.' That's what it said on the shiny brass plaque on his door.

I climbed the three flights of stairs to his top floor office, knocked and waited. He barked out for me to come in.

I walked into his office, the room stinking of the pipe he smoked all the time.

"Name? Form number? Have you a note? So you are interested in boy's anatomy are you? Or is it that you want to become a top boy, a big man? I see that you are in the top set. That will change if you continue in this manner. Well I will give you a lesson so you can go and tell all your little chums coming to see me, that it is no little boy's initiation ceremony. Let's make an example of you boy."

That must be why Seamus had done it. He must want to be in the dumb groups not the top ones. McGregor went and chose a cane from a rack on the wall.

"Now I think we need something substantial. I will not ask you to pull your trousers down. I would hate to see what I would find, so you are lucky in that respect. Bend over that chair boy. And grit your teeth."

The first thwack was horrible, a hot cutting pain. A few more whacks and he said "Are you going to do anything like this again boy? Answer me now."

I managed to say: "No sir."

"Well let's give you a few more reminders of this new-found educational knowledge." Another two swipes of the cane followed. Each time McGregor took his time to step back so he could hit me with full power. He was breathing hard now. "Will you be coming to see me again boy? Will you?"

"No sir."

McGregor sat down behind his desk.

"Next time it will be six. Just remember. Now get out of my sight."

The pain moved from my backside into the rest of my body. I left McGregor sitting behind his desk, banging the door on the way out. I thought I'd be in trouble for that, but I didn't care.

Going down the stairs to the playground wasn't easy. I walked out by the teachers' entrance and saw Seamus standing with fat Danny and some of his boys.

"Now hold up boys, here is someone who took one for the team. Well greebo, I told you not to stick your nose into my business but you've got the sore arse and I haven't."

Fat Danny stepped out from behind Seamus.

"Fucking hit him Seamus. I hate foreign fucks. Batter him."

Baz I couldn't take. He was big league, big time. But Fat Danny? Even though my arse hurt, I stood up on my toes, pulled my weight back and saying a few "malagas" and "pushdees," I let him have it. Right in his fat tum.

Fat Danny groaned as he doubled up.

Seamus laughed.

"Hey maybe you are alright Greebo. Next time you can be on my team eh?"

CHAPTER TWENTY FIVE

Mum shouted hello to me as I got in that night, in English.

"Zeno, is that you? I am watching Coronation Street but I want you to go to your room. There is something there for you."

I took my time going upstairs, I was still sore from the caning. And my hand hurt from punching Fat Danny.

On the bed were some new clothes. When I got closer I saw they were a pair of American jeans, proper ones with the bottoms rolled up. Pretty Boy Harry had a pair. There was also a jumper with a Zip, white with a blue pattern on the top, just like you saw on TV. And a new pair of grey school trousers, ones that weren't that horrible baggy material. The blue jeans were folded up with tissue paper in between them. I put them on but I didn't have to leave the top button undone. I put the jumper on, zipped halfway like I saw in all the American TV shows. The only mirror was in Maria's room so I went in there to look. This was really me. All I needed was one of those shirts without a collar on them.

I went downstairs.

"This time they fit just right Mum."

Mum laughed.

"You mean the Cyprus trousers. Sorry Zeno.

You know I can look at anybody and see their size. All my customers say only I can make them look good. Now I do it, the same for you."

She sat me down.

"Zeno I'm going to tell you that England is your home. This is the right place for you. And forget about Dad and his plans. He is just, oh what is the English word, missing home. You will help me Zeno do good in English, yes? From now on you and me will always speak English. Zeno why should you go back to Cyprus to cook souvlakia for tourists? You are better than that. You are a clever boy; your father doesn't see that. You should stay here and do something with your life. Become a teacher. Why not? I will not let your father make you live in some stinking village, without your family. Your brothers and sisters will not go. And I am not going there. I am making a good business with my clothes and perfume and it is getting bigger every week. Work hard at your school books Zeno and forget your Fathers plans."

"I can't go back there, I can't Mum."

"Was it so bad? There must have been things you liked?"

"Lots of bad things happened. Mum why didn't you tell me about my Uncle Zeno?"

Mum went quiet.

"Who told you about Zeno? One of the gossiping women I am sure. They have nothing better to do. Zeno this is why our life is here now. No more death and old stories."

"But there are the soldiers there Mum and the Turks and they don't like the Greeks and everybody is fighting each other. And then Stomei."

"Stomei? Now he really is a snake in the grass ready to bite. What did he do?"

"It was when I was running from goats, he showed me how to play chess but I was thirsty so he said for me to come in but then he gave me raki, I didn't drink it, I don't like the taste but then he..."

Mum came and sat by me.

"What did that stinking snake do Zeno? Can you say? Did he touch you?"

"He wanted me to touch his thing. You know. He got it out of his trousers, I didn't see it, I pushed him away and went up to see the soldiers."

"And your father? Where was he when all this was happening to you?"

"I didn't want to say anything because Dad was doing business with him. Will you tell Dad ?"

"Tell your father? There are things your father needs to know. You did well by telling me Zeno. Always tell me. There are bad people around, your Uncle Zeno God help us was bad in that way, but not with boys. This pushdee will have to pay for this."

"What will you do Mum?"

"Leave it to me. There is plenty we can do if he is still in Cyprus. Sotos can get very upset. But now let's go and see Dinos in his flat. There are things we need to say."

"Can I wear my new clothes?"

I half expected Mum to say they were only for best, but she said yes I could because there was no reason why I couldn't have lots of other new clothes. She could get them wholesale, which I guess meant cheap.

We walked slowly to the bus stop, I hoped to see some school friends, but there was nobody around. The jeans felt stiff and the legs scraped together, but I didn't care. Mum came upstairs with me instead of sitting with the old women and kids downstairs. We were even able to sit in the back because there were no smokers on the bus.

I hadn't been to Dinos flat since he moved in with his friends Albert and Dell. The flat was in a road with big old houses, it must be a house that had been divided up. When we got to Dinos' house there was a beautiful new blue and white two tone Cortina parked outside. It was the 'Deluxe' version, the blue stripe following the chrome strips down the sides to the round indicator lights. I didn't think it could belong to Albert or Dell and Dinos hadn't even passed his driving test so it couldn't be his. We pressed the bell to Flat four.

Albert, tall, skinny with a Teddy boy haircut opened the door with a smile.

"Hiya Mrs A and is that Zeno. Looking good boyo. Come in."

We pushed through the old bikes and shoes in the hall to the steamy kitchen.

Dell, small and slim was pulling something out of the cooker.

"Hi Mrs A. And Zeno. Haven't seen you in while, you've been in the wars, but looking good. I will have to watch out I'll have some competition at last." Dell fumbled with the tin can he had in his hand.

"Fuck, these bleeding tins get hot as hell, pardon me Mrs A. "

Albert fiddled around in a drawer and pulled out a rusty tin opener. "Don't mess your lovely little hands on these nasty tins. Anyway have you got shares in Frey Bentos? You're turning into a steak and kidney pie, Dell. Don't you ever have anything else?"

"I have chicken and mushroom pie some days. And get chips from the chippy sometimes as well."

"Yeah and you always get a pie then, too." Albert scraped his dinner onto a plate he had just washed. "At least I have some vegetables sometimes, like these beans."

Dell laughed. "Baked beans aren't a vegetable you wally."

"Well it's not a bleeding animal is it? It's not alive. You don't get beans running around the jungle eating each other do you? What do you think Zeno? Is a bean an animal or vegetable?"

Albert said to Dell: "Leave the boy alone. Go through Mrs A. You know who is here."

As we got closer I could hear voices in Dinos' room: Marias voice and one that I didn't recognise, a man's voice. We knocked and walked in. Now I knew who the voice belonged to. It was Call Me Steve. He was holding Maria's hand.

Maria got up. "Zeno, Mum. We didn't expect you." She came over to me.

"Zeno, this must be a bit of a surprise but me and Steve are, well you know together and Steve has asked me to marry him. I've said yes."

"Married? Cool. But you know I saw you. That time getting out of Steve's van. You kissed."

"You saw that and said nothing? Well done Zeno. That was good."

Steve reached into his pocket and gave me a two shilling coin.

"Thanks lad. That was a good thing to do. Appreciate it. Maybe you would like a ride in my new car, the Cortina ? We can go for a spin later."

Steve stood and shook Mum's hand. He gave me one of his winks. "Just let me know if there's anything I can do for you Zeno, anything."

The coin felt heavy in my hand.

"A Cortina? Cool. But what about Dad ? What will he say?"

We all looked at Mum.

"It is not what he will to us say but what we say to him that is important. Leave your father to me. I know what to do."

CHAPTER TWENTY SIX

A few weeks later, me and Dave had been at Mena's, practising saying ooh and shaking our heads to this new group called The Beatles. I was seeing lots of Meena now especially at school. She smelt as nice as Zash. And her eyes were warm and brown as well. I left Dave at his house, then I walked home singing: "Yeah, yeah, yeah."

I got to the corner by 'The Chocolate Box' sweet shop that Mr Patel had taken over from Old Sniffy. Patel had put his old Dad in the front of the shop on a stool just so he could watch all the boys that came in while his son served you. It made nicking any sweets almost impossible, but Dave said it was better than watching Old Sniffy's nose drip, hoping it would miss your sweets and drip onto the packet. I had some money from Steve; he often slipped me a few bob. Liquorice Allsorts or American wine gums? Which was it to be?

A figure stepped out of the alley by the shop. "Who loves you, yeah yeah? You think you can sing for your supper eh grease-ball? Well hold your breath because I need some exercise." Baz in full Teddy boy gear. His way of saying hullo was to let off a full, clenched fist punch right in my stomach. I realised now why it was a good idea to have some padding round my middle. Fat has a great way of soaking up pain. Often I groaned to let Baz know how hurt I was pretending to be. This time it was for real.

"I, er can't breathe. I can't..."

Baz grabbed me, tearing my new shirt as he pulled me to him.

"I don't care what you can't do. It's what you can do for me. Or you'll get more of this." He lifted me off the ground by the throat and pushed me against the wall, my feet dangling in space. "You've been avoiding me and that won't do. You think just because you've smartened yourself up you are as good as us. Well you're not. You are all still stinking, greasy eities that should fuck off back to the shithole that you came from."

I knew I was beaten. I had got good at fighting but I couldn't beat Baz.

"I've got money. Look here in my pocket. Half a crown. And some shillings."

Baz took the money and went to move away. Turning quickly he gave me one last slap on the face. My lip stung as I felt the warm trickle of blood begin to flow down my face. Baz turned to go. Laughing he gave me a final punch in my stomach. Bending over I fell to the ground panting for breath.

After what felt like a long time I looked up to see a large soldier, dressed in a green uniform. Beside him was a boy that I took a second to recognise. Salim!

Salim came over to me and took my hand.

"I knew it was you Zeno. As soon as I said to Dad he came straight over. What's happened to you?"

"He's your Dad? Wow. But how come you are

here?”

“Dad and Mum got a council house here because Dad is leaving the army to become a lorry driver.”

"So you're living here now?"

"Yes, starting school next week. Woodside."

"That's my school."

I got up slowly as Salim’s Dad lit one of those tight hand-made cigarettes that smell so sweet. He helped me up.

He said “Now Sunny Jim, you are the Greek boy that helped my Salim in Cyprus? What happened here?”

I told him all about Baz. Everything.

“Respect, that’s what’s missing today. Respect for elders and betters. That’s what he needs. A spell in The Army would do him some good. Just you show me who he is. He will soon find out not to mess with my son or any of his friends. I will speak his language. The only language a bully knows. ”

CHAPTER TWENTY SEVEN

"Mum, are you back to Greek again? You said English; I have to speak English to you."

"You know I don't know if I speak English or Greek now. I started talking Greek to Mavis, she said she didn't mind, she might go and visit Cyprus one day."

"The funny thing is, Mum, I'm doing the same thing, speaking Greek without knowing it."

We walked into the front room where Steve and Maria were sitting holding hands. Pedri was there too, the first time I'd seen him since coming back from Cyprus.

Pedri turned to me and whistled. "You have grown up fat boy. Nice kit too. Is that Mum's doing?"

I went and poked him in the shoulder.

"I'm not fat boy anymore ok? It's Zeno. That's what I'm called."

Pedri bunched his fist ready to slap me one until he saw the look in my face.

"You really have grown up fat er sorry Zeno. Respect. If I am coming to work here then yes I will call you Zeno."

I looked at Mum.

"Is Pedri coming back? Are we sharing rooms again? That's not what you said. You said..."

Mum came and gave me a hug.

"Pedri will come and work in the new shop, not live here again. I know that now. He can never live with us again. He has his own life."

I was confused.

"What new shop Mum?"

She turned to Steve.

"This is why we are here. Today Steve, you have to speak to my husband. You want to be a man, so this is your work. What are you going to say?"

"Well Mrs Antonio..."

"You can call me midera because I'm going to be your Greek mother. So talk."

"Well thank you Mrs... er midera."

Mum smiled.

"Masculine things end in an 'o' and all Greek feminine things end in 'a'. You will understand this soon, although sometimes things are complicated when a table is not either. But you will learn."

"Erm yes," Steve said. "Well, you see my plan is to use the success from your business and turn the cafe into a clothes shop. That way you wouldn't have to replace all the cooking equipment. I have a friend who is a builder and he would be happy to do the work because he owes me some favours and we can pay him with the profits."

Maria chipped in.

"The shop will also be a gentleman's alteration service. I know Dad doesn't like alteration work, but it's easy work and good money."

Steve nodded his head

"All my work colleagues say that the suits they buy often need something. The trousers are a bit too long or the coat buttons come off or one of the seams comes undone. There's nobody that can do that for them. I know a lot of people like that. I'm sure it will be a good business."

I was starving, proper hungry, not in that being full but still wanting to eat way, like I used to feel. I was just hungry. I really fancied a fried egg, the Greek way, fried in olive oil. The smell would remind me of the little kitchen in Cyprus, but it would never taste the same as the eggs we ate after collecting them first thing in the morning under the watch of Old Slit Eye.

I went to the kitchen to get the old black pan that Dad kept for frying eggs. They didn't stick to the bottom, like some of Mum's pans. If I was cooking a Greek style egg I wanted it on Greek style bread, plain with maybe a bit of the oil from the pan poured on the top and some salt, not like an English egg that would be fried in normal oil and put between two slices of white bread and maybe some brown sauce. Sometimes I liked it the English way and sometimes the Greek; not like Dad, always Greek, or Dave always English. I could like both.

As I started to fry the eggs, Dinos came into the kitchen. He must have been upstairs.

"That smells good Zeno. What about doing some for all of us, Greek Cypriot style?"

"Sure Den. But what's that shirt you're wearing? It's not one of Mum's is it?"

"No I wouldn't be seen dead in that crap. No

this is genuine Indian, things are changing boy. Cuba is the place to be, it's all happening there. We need to change the world to help the oppressive masses. Anyway you'd better get cracking. Ha! So that's me, Mum, you, Maria, Steve and Pedri."

I told Dinos that I'd sort it. Get the eggs; make sure there is a spare one, just in case. Always the Greek way is to make a little bit more. You never know who might come at the last minute. Now to cut the Greek bread, no butter, the olive oil would be enough. I loved how the eggs bubbled and spluttered as the white got thicker. I got the plates organised and some of the serviettes from the café, one for each plate. Mine was ready so I took a bite out of it, the yolk dribbling out the sides, just as I liked it.

The door downstairs banged: Dad's heavy feet. I put a sandwich carefully on a plate and went into the front room. Dad was standing looking at Steve. He spoke to Mum in Greek.

"What is this boy doing here? Why have you invited him into my house?"

Mum replied in English.

"We will speak so everybody understands. Speak English. This boy is to marry Maria. And he will be the one that saves this family."

"Save the family? Everything is gone. What is there to save? If we could have gone to Cyprus then maybe..."

"No more Cyprus Manolli. This is where we are now. Nobody will go back. You dream. Always you dream. But you don't see what is in front of you. Your children have grown up without you noticing. Only Zeno is young. But you do not keep him safe. Tell him, Zeno. Tell your Father what happened."

Dad turned to me standing by the door.

"Well Zeno. Now that you have found your voice. What have you to say about me being a bad Father?"

The room was quiet. I started mumbling about Uncle Zeno, Salim, Fanoulla. I didn't say anything about Stomei.

Dad shook his head.

"I will start with the one who speaks the most sense. Maria, why is this man here?"

Maria looked at Steve. Although Dad still spoke Greek, Steve knew this was his time to speak. He stood up and cleared his throat.

"Sir, er Mr Antionou. I am here at your wife's invitation to ask for the hand of your daughter to do me the honour of being my wife. I love her very much sir, I will make her very happy. Really."

Dad turned away from Steve.

"Maria. Do you want this boy for your husband? What do we know about his family, his blood? He is not part of us, we know nothing about him. How could your Mother have allowed this? She should be looking after you not painting her face and selling dresses to stupid women."

It was Dinos turn to stand up. I hope it wasn't going to be a lecture about Cuba. We had a lot of that recently.

"Dad, you can't talk about Mum like that. She has kept the family going while you were pissing around in Cyprus. Nobody wants to go back and you can't make us. And Steve is a decent bloke. He can fix the shop up and everything."

"Fix up the shop? You mean the Café? This boy has so much money that he will spend it on the Café? Why would he do that?"

Mum went and held Marias' hand.

"It won't be a café. No more Manolli. No more food and grease and washing up. Steve will fix it as a clothes shop. I can sell to women. You can do alterations. It could be a good business. Maria will live with Steve's parents, they have a big house, Dinos is away now and Pedri too."

"Pedri. Always Pedri. That boy..."

"I'm not a boy!" Pedri's turn to stand up. "And I can do what I want, I don't need to listen to you. All you do is talk about what you want. You never listen and..."

Mum went over to Pedri.

"That's enough now. Your Father needs respect. He tries hard for all of you. Now everybody is to go. Here take some money for a Chinese. Go to Dinos's flat. Your Father and me have to talk. Now Zeno you want to say anything?"

I looked at dad and all the family in the room. Holding the plate up I said "Egg sandwich anybody?"

Later, after I went to bed, Dad came and woke me up.

"Is it true Zeno? I cannot sleep. That pushdee Stomei. Your Mother told me. If he ever comes back to England, he will pay. "

Sighing he came and sat on the chair next to my bed.

"I have been just like my Father, God rest his drunken bones. I only think of my own words. Your mother is right. We are here in England. To stay. And this business your mother is planning. Yes it could be a good business. And I can save my good food for the people that like it. My own family. "

He stood up smacking one fist into another like he wanted to punch someone.

"Next year we will go back and make sure of Stomei. Now I will send a letter to Sotos that Stomei won't like."

"It's okay Dad. I made sure nothing happened. Cyprus was all right. I mean, there were some good bits."

He looked at me, then nodded and chuckled.

"I want you to know the ... um... good bits. Maybe next year, we will go for a holiday. Your Mother will come and Maria and her new husband. A family. What do you think Zeno? Uh?"

Dad really wanted me to like Cyprus. As long as we were all together, I didn't care.

"Yes Dad," I said. "I will go back with you next summer. Back to Cyprus."

19071977R00099

Printed in Poland
by Amazon Fulfillment
Poland Sp. z o.o., Wrocław